SEER OF EPERA

CHRISTINE CAZALY

Contents

Chapter One

Epera, Castle of Air, Easter 1567

From her Book of Shadows – Theda of the Owls, Seer of Epera

My teacher always told me when the Mage speaks, you will listen.

But there are times when I wish he would not speak.

And many more times when I wish I could not hear.

High in the north of Altius Mysterium, in the chilly northern kingdom of Epera, a soft spring sunset gilded the snowcapped tops of the Iron Mountains with gold and painted the peaceful evening sky in stripes of pink and lilac. Busy birds wheeled and called to each other as they glided to roost in the vast forests that decorated the deep valleys and lower slopes. The starlings that lived at the Castle of Air gathered and swirled, sketching black ribbons against their magnificent canvas. Retiring with the sun, they folded their wings in the towers and battlements of the magnificent, ancient building that guarded the pass to the ore-rich mountains. Their raucous chatter marked the end of the working day for its human inhabitants, who glanced up from their chores and thought of supper.

Hunched over her work at a polished oak desk in front of the vast fireplace, Theda of the Owls, Seer of Epera, scrubbed an ink-stained hand through her hair and raised her head, squinting in the increasing gloom as the sun slipped lower in the sky, and the natural light faded.

Her domain, the immense library of the Castle of Air, stretched into a seemingly endless distance on either side of her. Books, scrolls and papers crowded the stacks, jostling for attention and space. Tall shelves lined the long room, running off at perpendicular angles from the central aisle on both sides. The gaps in between formed small, intimate spaces that played host to scholars, teachers and students alike. A further mezzanine floor, equally crowded and reached by ornate, curving stairwells, hugged the upper storey. A row of majestic, many-paned windows stretched down one long side. The view to the western mountains over the crenelated ramparts and grey stone walls of the castle was stunning, but, generally, the population of the Great Library of Epera were too busy arguing with each other to notice.

A gentle murmur of intense conversation whispered across the space, punctuated now and then by raised voices or bursts of laughter. Theda allowed herself a smile as she stretched the kink out of her back. Lessons for the young, both Citizen and Blessed, had almost completed for the day, and the voices of the students at their studies were giving way to comments about the possibilities on offer at the evening meal and the progress of the Queen's pregnancy.

"Master Skinner, the lights, if you please," she called, catching the eye of one of her colleagues in the alcove opposite her perch.

The man flashed a smile and rose to his feet with dapper grace. The small class of six-year-olds who comprised the group around his table waited, eyes lit with enthusiasm, as he shook back the long sleeves of his robe. Theda shook her head at the display. Robert Skinner was one of her closest colleagues, but he never could resist the temptation to put on a show. He nodded at her, blue eyes creasing with laughter at the corners, long, greying hair tousled around the fur of his collar, and flicked his pale, fine-boned fingers right and left.

The children let out an "ooh!" of amazement while a series of ironic cheers from more jaded students echoed around the long room. Robert smirked as the lanterns placed strategically on the desks and on the ends of the stacks blazed to life under his mental command, and the titles of the newer volumes picked out in gold shimmered from their shelves.

Theda rolled her eyes as he shook out his sleeves with a theatrical bow and regained his seat. "Yes, yes, very good," she said, picking up her quill once more and dipping it carefully in ink.

She was interrupted five short sentences later.

"I've finished sorting the shelves in the history section."

"We are due to supper." Theda glanced up again. The young man lounged patiently before her, one lock of jet-black hair twisted absently across his forehead, hands held loosely at his sides. He shifted his weight, eyes dark as pitch in the yellow light of the lanterns as his gaze travelled hungrily over a row of books waiting on a wooden trolley to be shelved. He was handsome enough already, but the soft light flattered him further. Edged his high cheekbones with gold, and breathed warmth into his skin that, seen in the daylight, was paler than snow. He was exceptionally tall, with the promise of great strength to come in the breadth of his shoulders and the weight in his bones. A dagger boasting a richly bejewelled hilt hung from a finely tooled leather scabbard at his narrow waist. He wore a flat red hat with a drooping falcon feather and a fine velvet tunic. Too fine, really, to be toiling in the library. He unleashed a smile. A more deadly weapon than his dagger. Even Theda found it hard to resist.

"You may shelve these. I want them all done, though. No stopping to read them before supper."

He sketched a bow and withdrew with the trolley down the rows, iron wheels squeaking.

Conscious of her growling stomach, Theda shoved her chair back from her desk and stood, marking his progress from under her brows as he disappeared around a corner. The wheels stopped squeaking, and she shook her head. He would scan the contents of every title before placing it carefully back on the shelf. She'd never known a scholar like him. Other young men had to be chased around the castle to attend their studies. That one never stopped.

Lessons finished for the day. Released from their tedium, children scampered away. The older scholars strolled out in small groups, still discussing their theories. Many smiled and nodded as they passed her desk. Theda busied herself tidying her papers and only looked up when a shadow fell across her light.

"Will you supper with me, Mistress Eglion?" Robert Skinner asked.

"That would be enjoyable. I thank you."

Distracted, her gaze drifted back to the stacks, where the sound of squeaking wheels once again marked her assistant's progress.

"Are you well? You look a little pale."

Robert retrieved her cloak from the back of her chair and placed it carefully over her narrow shoulders against the chill of the corridors.

Theda shrugged off his concern.

"Quite well, Robert. I slept but little last night, that is all, and I expect Briana to arrive from Blade at any moment. She should be in time for the evening meal."

How could she tell her colleague of her vision from the midnight hours, jumping from slumber, sweat beading her brow and heart banging in fright? What to say about the image of his dead body or the hard faces of iron-clad soldiers herding groups of the Blessed into a remote and unknown darkness? Better he knew her only as a Citizen and Chief Librarian, famed for her reputation as a scholar, with an eligible daughter, and not as a member of the Blessed, the greatest Seer of her generation. The future was a twisty thing. Shaded and carved and ribboned with a million different choices. And her God, the Mage, parcelled out his wisdom sparingly. In glimpses, on the edges of reflections, in dreams and nightmares. The Mage had chosen a dark future to show her last night; that was all.

Comforted by Robert's care and the richness of his baritone as he continued to chat, she took the guiding elbow he offered and allowed him to escort her along the magnificent corridors of the vast Castle of Air. A beguiling mixture of warmth, music and the rich smell of roasting meat bellied around them as they neared the Great Hall, luring them in with a blaze of candles and, as ever, the promise of gossip.

Chapter Two

From the journal of Briana of the Owls, Whitethorn Manor, March 1567

At last, I can join my mother at the centre of magic in Epera! Three years of learning, seclusion and study at my grandmother's freezing manor are enough for anyone and if some dried up old crone ever again says "pay more attention," I will probably have to kill them. They say the King honours the most powerful of the Blessed at the Court of the Skies, and my mother is surely the greatest of these. The Seer of Epera. Perhaps her staff will come to me one day, if I am worthy, and the Mage wills it.

Two strong armed members of the King's Servers stood at attention on either side of the solid oak and iron-studded doors that opened onto the vast room where the Court of Air met to eat, drink and play.

One of the largest rooms in the Castle of Air, the dominant feature of the Great Hall was its famed hammer beam ceiling. Rich, colourful tapestries warmed the walls next to the enormous fireplace. Opposite it, two tall, narrow windows, paned with rippled glass, gave a stunning view across Smokethorn valley and onto the mountains beyond.

Four long tables led to the King's dais that bisected them at the far end. Presently, it was empty. The royal family had yet to make an appearance. Theda and Robert performed the traditional obeisance to the Throne that was required as they entered, and Robert guided her to a bench at the second table about halfway down the board. The courtier to her left nodded dismissively and turned pointedly away to his female companion. Theda rolled her eyes. Robert had seated them amongst the Blessed, and, despite her reputation as a scholar, King Francis's court regarded her as a Citizen. The distinction shouldn't be as profound, but here, in the castle, the difference was obvious and scrupulously observed. Francis' disdain for those not Blessed with magical ability was famous. And where the King's mind lay, there the court followed. Robert poured wine into her pewter goblet, and she raised it to her lips, smoothing the frown lines from her face with an effort.

A few minutes later, the company swayed to its collective feet and bowed as the King entered on a blast of trumpets, supporting his sovereign Queen, Gwyneth, on his arm. He nodded right and left. Piercing blue eyes, deep-set under an aging brow, flashed around the assembly. Famed throughout the continent for his quick mind and decisive nature, he still had the power to terrify when his concentrated gaze turned towards an unlucky miscreant. A plain steel crown circled his head. His robes, rich dark blue, lined with ermine, broadened his frame. Amongst the Blessed at the Court of Air, Francis claimed the power of the Eagles. Gossip said he could leave his body and fly with that noble bird over the tops of mountains. Few believed it.

His young wife, Gwyneth, of neighbouring Oceanis, smiled at the court, her green eyes serene as she made slow progress to the dais.

Swollen to vast proportions in late pregnancy, her stomach led the way. Theda smiled at King Francis' care of his beloved as he handed her to her seat and helped her to wine from a silver flagon. A favoured group of waiting serfs served the King, and he started his meal, nodding to the court staff, who began a long process of serving food to the ranks of the court. Theda's mouth watered as the rich aroma of meat and gravy wafted towards her. The tables and benches shuddered as people regained their seats, and the conversation picked up to its usual ear-splitting level.

"Not long now, before the Queen gives birth," Robert remarked, helping himself to meat from the platter that a servant had left on the table in front of them. He lifted a pewter jug of wine and waved it at her. "Want some more?"

Theda nodded her thanks.

"It is admirable how he is with her," she said, filling her trencher with gravy. "Stern as he is, I would never have thought it."

"He waited long enough to take a bride, and he certainly seems smitten with her. How long before Briana arrives?"

"I received a bird from her this morning. She is on her way. I hope she arrives in time to eat."

"You will look forward to seeing her after all this time, no doubt."

"I have missed her," Theda admitted, slicing roast boar with her eating knife and, at last, transferring it to her mouth.

Robert chewed thoughtfully and nodded in recognition as he swallowed his meat and reached for more wine.

"It is hard to leave them in the care of their nurses, but I believe it is even harder to when they return, older and wiser, as they think," he said, blue eyes twinkling.

Theda laughed. "You should know! How are your boys doing?"

"Terrence is studying architecture. He wants to build the greatest Temple to the Mage that Epera has ever seen. Mattias is for the army. Not a Blessed bone in his body."

"Other than quick wits, great speed, and the talent for gossip that we are all gifted with here in Epera," Theda rejoined dryly.

Robert nodded an acknowledgment, and Theda turned her attention to her meal. There had been no bird from Briana, of course. Just a quick mental message accompanied by a burst of excitement at the prospect of life at court. Theda's shoulders contracted under her thick woollen gown. Briana would not like what Theda had to tell her.

The meal over, sweating servants cleared the tables and shifted the long benches to the walls. The court grouped together in their usual factions. Blessed to one side of the room, Citizens to the other. Scholars and scientists of all stripes formed another thick knot, distinguishable by their shabbiness, contrasted by the rich velvets and furs of the chattering nobility. Theda's foot tapped automatically as young Girdred, the most talented musician the court could boast, began a lively jig and people chose partners for the dance.

Clutching another glass of wine, taking little part in the conservation, Theda's eyes turned time and again to the doorway, anticipating her daughter's russet head and snapping grey eyes. They had not seen each other for three years. Briana was seventeen now. Time to seek a partner for her. And where better than the castle, where she could have her pick of the court?

A prickle of magical apprehension gripped her mind as her gaze travelled absently around the throng to land on the tall figure of her library assistant, who must have succumbed to hunger after all. Brow quirking as he strolled across the hall, she noticed how he straightened his stance and squared his shoulders, pausing now and then to converse with the Citizens of his acquaintance. His smile dazzled.

He lingered for a quick joke here, a whispered conversation in the delicate ear of another maiden there. People watched him from the corners of their eyes as he passed. Darius of Falconridge. recent heir to a fortune, the second most favoured family in the land. His mother, long dead, had been Blessed with the rare art of Mind-walking. His father's Blessed gift of telekinesis had rivalled Robert Skinner's.

The Mage had Blessed Darius with nothing at all. As far as she was aware, immense charm and a massive appetite for obscure knowledge did not count.

The young man left the small group of courtiers closest to the dais. Queen Gwyneth rested uncomfortably on her wooden backed chair, hands clasped protectively around her unborn child, surrounded by the ladies of her household. They clapped in time to the music as Francis joined the group of dancers. Francis offered his hand to his partner, the elderly Countess of Goldfern, who curtsied with arthritic grace. Music swirled into a flourish, and the attention of the court rested on its ruler as he performed the intricate steps of a slow pavane with somewhat stiff-legged precision.

Darius approached the dais and reached into the pocket of his tunic. Extracting a scroll of parchment, bound with an emerald-green ribbon, he went down on one knee in front of the Queen, who focused a tired and gentle smile on his hopeful boyish face.

She took the parchment he held out to her automatically and unwound the ribbon, smoothing it carefully in her long fingers. Her eyes scanned the script. Was it only Theda who noticed as her gaze sharpened at the words written there before she schooled her expression and handed the page back to him with a courtly smile and a shake of her head?

Face lowered, the young man retreated from the Queen's presence. He still appeared relaxed as he rejoined his companions, although a bloom of rose heated his pale cheeks. Theda frowned. Queen Gwyneth, with her sun hued hair, green eyes and soft smile, received poems and missives like the one Darius had undoubtedly just offered her all the time. Her constant refusal to accept them only resulted in renewed competition from the young courtiers to win her favour in the game of courtly love. So far, she had adamantly refused to extend it, treating all her admirers with the same gentle forbearance. Eyes narrowed, Theda watched Darius lean closer to his friends. A rush of malicious laughter erupted between them, followed closely by a tumult of head shaking and theatrical expressions of concern.

Unaccountably nervous, Theda's eyes flickered to the doorway once more, and she jumped when Robert materialised at her side.

He smiled. "My pardon, Mistress, your thoughts are far away."

Theda managed a ragged smile for him. "Tonight, I find my thoughts are far from peaceful," she admitted.

Another burst of laughter exploded from Darius' friends, and her shoulders twitched with irritation. Nothing felt right tonight. Her skin prickled like a cat's fur rubbed the wrong way. The surrounding conversation bled into her senses, first too loud, then a mere murmur, hard to hear. Her head whirled. The Mage was grappling for her attention. There was something here, in this room, that was important. What was it?

"Briana will be here soon, do not fear."

Robert's voice was soft, and his long-fingered hand on her sleeve brought with it a measure of comfort.

"Dance with me?"

"Really, I..."

"Do not tell me you cannot dance. I will not believe it. Not in one so graceful."

He reached for her hand, and Theda let him lead her into the galliard. She performed the intricate steps automatically, a smile fixed on her face that gave the lie to the restless thoughts behind it. They were nearing the end of the last measure when, at last, she heard it.

The King is not the babe's father.

She stumbled, covering the misstep with a low curtsey. Robert helped her to her feet with a perplexed frown as the music blared its conclusion, and she returned to her place at the edge of the room.

"Are you well, Mistress?"

Theda gazed up at him, but she couldn't see the concern in his expression. His face blurred in her vision, and a sudden start of tears saw her reaching for a kerchief and blotting her eyes under the guise of wiping perspiration from her clammy forehead. Impossible to tell whether she had really heard the words, or just picked up the thoughts of someone else in the company.

"Mistress? Shall I escort you to your rooms?"

The king is not the father.

The words slammed into her ears again, and she whirled, trying to place the speaker. Whoever it was, this was treason. If the King should hear it, there would be blood on the flags.

"Robert, did you hear that?"

"What?"

"What someone is saying about the Queen... the babe?"

Robert looked at her as if she had run mad.

"'T'is warm in here. Let me take you out. Get some air."

"No, I..."

Panicked, she sat, transfixed, as the King returned to his seat, bending low to whisper in the Queen's ear. The soft sound of her laughter trickled across the room, and she patted her husband's hand. He caught her fingers and pressed a kiss to them.

Tall in the crowd, her gaze snared once again on her library assistant. He was staring at the Queen, wistful and defiant and righteous all at once, fingering the scroll he had presented to her so optimistically. His pale cheeks flushed as the Queen laughed and Theda flinched at the fierceness with which he crushed the heavy parchment that declared his love.

Jealous. Theda realised suddenly. Whatever Darius felt for her, it was more than just courtly love.

Head held high, Darius bid his friends a good night and left the room. Troubled though she was, Theda's heart shot to the heavens as he moved sideways in the doorway, bowing with scrupulous manners to make way for a newcomer.

Briana had arrived.

Chapter Three

From the journal of Briana of the Owls

The journey from Blade is long and steeply uphill. The horse strains to pull our carriage up the last piece of rutted road. By the Gods, the Castle of Air is huge. Its mossy grey walls fill the sky like a lowering fist. I should be happy to be here. I am happy to be here, at the Court of Skies, where the most powerful of the Blessed attend the king.

But look how the birds circle the turrets. Look how high the battlements and the thousand candle-lit windows, and the fluttering banners with the King's eagle flying in the chill wind from the mountains. The Castle of Air has a face of stone. Will I be happy here?

Face wreathed in an unaccustomed smile, Theda hurried across the room to her daughter.

Briana stood on the threshold, hands akimbo on her hips, the hood of her cloak forming a striking backdrop for her dark red curls, crystal grey eyes alight with curiosity as she surveyed the crowd.

"Briana! At last!"

Her daughter smiled and extended her arms. Theda crushed the girl to her heart. Briana smelled of spring air, sunshine, and daffodils.

"Mother! It has been so long."

They parted and regarded each other, hands clasped.

"Have you eaten? I have something in our chambers. The main meal is over."

"I could do with something to eat," Briana said. "I'm starving. Who's that?"

Theda stood back as Robert Skinner strolled over, a welcoming smile spread across his wide mouth.

"Well, well, the daughter has arrived. Your mother has been on pins for days," he informed her, holding out a fresh goblet of wine. "Robert Skinner, a tutor in your mother's library at your service. Come, meet some people."

He extended an elbow to Briana, who stepped forward, reaching for the wine, eagerness in every line of her.

"Briana." Theda's hand shot out to catch her daughter's arm.

"May I not just..."

Theda's tone sharpened. "We have matters to discuss, Briana, before your entry to the Court of Skies. Come now. Eat, rest."

Her command brooked no disobedience, and Briana's features contracted with sudden disappointment. She withdrew her arm.

"As you wish, Mother."

She curtsied to Master Skinner, who bowed and returned to his friends, throwing Theda a questioning glance as he went.

Theda preceded her daughter away from the crowded banqueting hall and along wide corridors punctuated at intervals by suits of armour and lit by torches. Priceless tapestries depicting the sign of the Mage and stories of the Four Great Gods and the making of the world decorated the stone walls. Briana stared at them, openmouthed, as they passed by under the stern eyes of the immortals.

"We are in the west wing on the second floor," Theda informed her daughter. "We have a set of chambers with a view over the tiltyards."

"Why won't you let me stay downstairs?"

Briana's mental question drummed an insistent note in Theda's brain. She shook her head.

"I will explain in just a moment."

Briana said no more until they were safely in their small suite, and Theda had locked the door behind them. A castle servant had already delivered Briana's luggage. It stood in a small, battered heap on the vividly patterned rug in front of the fire. Briana took off her cloak and looked around. Theda followed her curious gaze, wondering what their sanctuary must look like to her daughter. They were lucky. It was a small suite with its own fireplace and a fine view. The beds were comfortable, covered by woolen blankets. She had a carpet, pewter utensils. A small table, two chairs upholstered in faded tapestry. It was a good suite for a Citizen.

Theda indicated a door that led to a further chamber. "Your room is through there," she said. "We don't have an allotted servant, so we will make our own fires and tend to our own needs. We take meals every forenoon and evening in the Great Hall. You will help me in the library whilst you are here."

"No servants? Do the Blessed not warrant them here? And why such small rooms? You are the Seer of Epera, surely the King..."

Theda cut her off with a quick wave of her hand.

"The King is aware of the Seer of Epera, of course, but we have never met in person," she said. "Here, in the Castle of Air, I am Mistress Eglion, Chief Librarian. That is all."

Briana blinked, astonished. "A Citizen?" she asked.

Theda raised a quelling eyebrow and gave her a single, grim nod.

"By all the Gods, why?"

Theda grimaced. That was a good question.

"The Mage..." she started.

Briana slumped onto the nearest chair and folded her arms over her head. "Oh, no. don't tell me." Her long sleeves muffled her voice.

"Don't be ridiculous, Briana." Theda's tone was sharper than she had intended. She busied herself at the table, cutting up an apple, rich Argentian cheese, and a small loaf of bread with quick, precise strokes of her eating dagger. "Here. Eat."

She put a platter in her daughter's lap. Briana caught it before it slid to the floor.

Theda poured wine for them both and took a chair opposite as Briana consumed her supper. Exasperated as she was, the sight of her only precious offspring, here in the chamber with her, eating a meal, filled her heart with joy. She took a grateful sip of wine and regarded her daughter over the rim.

"There are bad times coming, Briana," she said.

Briana paused, mid-bite. "What bad times?"

Theda sighed. "As ever, the way is not clear. The Mage has shown me trouble coming to the Blessed. I feel it is creeping closer, but I cannot be sure from which direction it will come, what form it takes, or what the outcome will be. I fear Master Skinner is in great danger, although I cannot warn him. He thinks I am a mere Citizen. I am careful to keep any of them from thinking otherwise."

"So, I am here, at your request, at a place where the Blessed are almost as powerful as the Gods, but I cannot use my gift? You expect me to present myself at court as an ordinary Citizen, to be looked down upon and ignored? What will I do?"

Exasperated, Theda's eyebrows contracted in a fierce frown. "This is about more than you and your ego, my girl. You will not do what we both know you can do. Not unless you are here, in the privacy of our chambers. No one in this castle must know you as anything other than a beautiful, intelligent young woman. You will keep a guard on your mind at all times. I must protect you, Briana. At some point, it will not be safe to be known as a member of the Blessed."

Briana scoffed, throwing back her curls. "I'm not a child, mother. I am Blessed. One of the most powerful in the land. Who could harm me?"

She glanced at her half-eaten supper and waved a casual hand. Theda rolled her eyes as the contents of the platter renewed at her daughter's command. The butter returned to its neat pat, the apple, half-eaten, now whole, red and rosy on its dish. The nibbled cheese a single, fragrant block.

Triumphant, eyes alight like two grey pebbles in a sparkling stream, Briana met her mother's stare.

"You see, mother. What I can do?" She waved her hand again. Her travelling garb, dusty with drying mud, became a court gown in deep garnet red, complete with a headdress studded with rubies.

"Illusion and transformation. I know, Briana."

Theda crouched in front of her daughter and caught the delicate hand that commanded one of the rarest gifts the Mage bestowed. To her knowledge, Briana was the only member of the Blessed who possessed it.

"You have great power, my daughter. But as with all our gifts, it is not what we have but how we choose to use them, for good or for ill."

Briana scowled, and her hand slithered like silk from Theda's grasp.

"You always say that."

"Because it is true. Of all the gifts, yours is the most rare. It is also the most laden with temptation to misuse."

"I won't misuse it. It won't control me. I know that's what you are worried about."

Eyes narrowed, Theda skewered her only child in place with a steely glare. The atmosphere in the room took on the charged quality of the sky before a storm as their iron wills clashed.

"Beware, girl. Your pride could mark your downfall." Theda's soft words tumbled through the space between them like drifting snowflakes, stinging with cold as they landed. Undaunted, Briana raised her chin, cloud grey eyes reflecting the firelight as she threw the words back.

"Beware, mother mine. Your need to control everything around you could be yours."

Theda's gaze darkened. She stood, her eyes drifting to the closed door of her bedchamber, where she had woken only a few hours earlier, sweating, screaming with terror.

"As you will, daughter, but know this. Master Skinner is Blessed as well. A man from a humble background with powerful magic. Much respected. Well known." She took another sip of wine. It slipped over her teeth like acid.

"But a few hours ago, the Mage showed me a very clear image of his corpse, covered with blood and bruises, hanging on a rope.

Chapter Four

From the journal of Briana, of the Owls

I can't use my magic, she says. Once again, the word of the Mage takes all the fun out of life. It's ridiculous. What's the use of being here, one of the most powerful Blessed in Epera, if all I end up doing is mouldering in the library, and taking supper with the Citizens?

After a long day in the library, teaching Eperan history to children of the nobility, Theda was more than ready for the evening meal. Robert Skinner rose with his usual grace at dusk to light the lamps, and Theda went in search of her daughter. Tired of Briana's continual, low voiced griping, and her dreadful handwriting, she'd sent the girl into the stacks with a trolley load of books and not seen her since.

Rounding a corner into the history section, Theda paused, cloak swirling around her ankles. The tinkle of Briana's laughter grated on her ears. Theda strained her magical senses, but, as instructed, and despite her complaints, Briana had closed her mental channels. Her thoughts did not leak from her in a way that Theda could pick up.

Darius, in profile, smiled politely and took the book Briana handed to him, reaching over her to shelve it. He moved away, but Briana's pale hand closed on his brocade sleeve, preventing his escape. Theda shook her head.

"Briana!" she called. "The evening meal will shortly be served. Are you ready?"

"Coming, mother."

Briana's tone was pleasant enough, and she was smiling as she strolled down the stacks to where Theda drummed her fingers against the shelves.

"What's the matter?" she asked, as the two turned and left the library. "I am just being nice to that boy. He's got no magic. Just like me." The emphasis her daughter placed on the last three words left Theda in no doubt that a game was being played. She tightened her jaw. She'd blast the gods before she would give the little minx the satisfaction.

"Lord Darius of Falconridge is not for you," she said, keeping her temper with an effort.

"He's a Lord? He's nice." Briana turned her face away, pretending interest in the dull metal of a suit of armor.

"Believe me, despite that lovely smile, and charming manners, he'd be more interested in you if you grew pages and bled ink." Theda stifled a chuckle at the shock on her daughter's face. "He's a scholar, through and through. Not a courtier. He'd pay you no attention and bore you in a month."

"I'm bored now." Briana said.

"No, you are not. You can't be. You are in the Court of Skies. There is always something to do. Someone to talk to."

"It's no fun without magic."

"You will get to know some Citizens, tonight. Associating with them won't do you any harm. They are perfectly acceptable people."

Briana rolled her eyes, and Theda stifled a sigh. Time had passed, and the day was long gone when she could command her wilful offspring to obey with just the force of her glare.

The King was already in attendance as they entered the Great Hall. The Queen's chair stood vacant, the ladies of her household nowhere to be seen. All eyes rested on the king, who perched on his seat like a bird about to take flight, concern written across his creased face. Gossip swept the hall even as Theda and Briana took a couple of spaces at a board far down the row, clustered with Citizens, who, whilst unable to perform magic, still chattered like starlings.

"The Queen is in labour."

"I heard she had pains after dinner last night."

"Prince or Princess, d'ye think? I wager a sovereign 'tis a lad."

"My mother, Theodora, is a member of the queen's household. She told me the Queen was feeling unwell this morning." Ariana of Wessendean, the young woman seated to Briana's left, glanced around at her immediate neighbours, her face smug with the flush of one with more than second hand gossip to share. Blonde curls bobbed around a neck as white and smooth as marble, wrapped in a scarlet ribbon. An unfortunate choice, to Theda's mind. She looked as if someone had taken a knife to her throat.

Nods of acknowledgement followed her statement, and the nearest courtiers returned to their meal, conversing in low voices, speculating on the King's reaction to his newborn child.

"Her child is not the king's."

Hand arrested in midair as she reached for a loaf of bread, Theda stiffened as the last comment batted her ears, just as it had the night before. Her head snapped around, looking for the whisperer. Further up the table, Darius's group of cronies crowded together, sharing a flagon of ale. Darius himself was nowhere to be seen.

She sat back, confused, as the whisper started up again. "...Not his child, not his child. The queen has played him false." For a few heartbeats, she almost wondered if she was imagining it.

Theda dropped her bread to the board and watched, transfixed, as the dreadful rumour floated like feathers from a split pillow across the massed courtiers. With her heightened senses, she could almost feel the words as a physical presence, coiling like a viper around gossiping tongues, poisoning the atmosphere as they travelled. It was only a matter of time before the rumour reached the King. She blanched, watching as faces changed, and the tenor of the conversation altered, shifted. Grew teeth.

"Mother, are you alright?" Briana's soft voice in her ear sounded very far away. "Mother?"

Two tables away. She could do nothing to prevent him from hearing it. Her pulse thudded a warning beat in her ears.

One table away. This was it. This was the terrible thing. The start. The blade she had so dreaded was about to fall. She dropped her hands to her lap under the table, fingers twisted in agitation as perspiration prickled across her shoulders.

The King heard.

His face changed, first white with shock, a trickle of doubt, then overcome with rage. His eyes snapped from courtier to courtier, who did not have the courage to meet his glare.

Scraping back his heavy chair with a screech like nails across glass, he leaned over the cowering nobles like a vengeful god. The heavy ring that dominated his right hand flared to life and sent shards of white light across the company, who flinched as it found them. The Ring of Justice. Symbol of the King's absolute and Blessed right to rule.

"Who dares?" He roared, so loud his voice rattled the ancient windows and blew dust from the distant candelabra hanging from the ancient oak beams. "Who dares question the paternity of my child? Who dares question the integrity of my sovereign lady? Let him come forth! Come forth now, I say, and tell me this to my face!"

Silence. Theda glanced around. The Court of Skies suddenly appeared exceptionally interested in the contents of their platters.

The king's gaze continued to rove across the company, searching for the gossipmonger. Theda was one of the few people who noticed a small door open to admit Theodora of Wessendean, a senior member of the Queen's household. She entered the chamber from the rear of the room, behind the king's dais, and tapped her way across the flags, face serious under her greying curls. The charged atmosphere in the room did not pass her by. The woman's gaze flicked around the terrified courtiers to land on King Francis and she quailed visibly, looking for support. There was none to be had, and apparently, her case was urgent. Theda had never had much time for the woman, but she found a moment to admire her courage as Theodora swallowed heavily and made her approach.

"What?"

King Francis spat the question at the woman as she performed a shaky curtsey to him.

"Your Majesty, the Queen is in distress. We have sent for her physicians."

Theda's shoulders relaxed momentarily as the atmosphere shifted once more, and the King released his stranglehold on his courtier's wits.

He nodded curtly to the company, who stumbled to their feet to salute his departure as he swept from the hall, face still twisted with rage.

In his wake, a tidal wave of conversation broke, and the terrible gossip swelled once more.

"Surely the king does not believe idle court chit chat?" Briana asked, reaching once more for her meal.

Theda swallowed, sorting through the impressions that tumbled through her mind. Imperative amongst them was the need to remain incognito. Now more than ever. The Seer of Epera knew something important had taken place. Mistress Eglion, Citizen, would know much less.

"I do hope not, daughter. Let us hope the queen is well, and her child too."

She nodded repressively to Briana, who bit her lip to swallow her next inappropriate question before it left her tongue.

"The queen longs to be a mother," Ariana said, tearing bread with small, sharp teeth and mumbling through it. "My mother says..."

"Your mother says entirely too much. Finish your meal." Theda snapped.

Ariana turned wounded doe eyes to her and Theda glared at her until the girl turned away to talk to Briana.

Briana's expression held questions as she listened absently to her neighbour. Theda nodded faintly in her direction. In other circumstances, she and Briana would talk about this to each other through their mental connection. But for now, the conversation would have to wait. As her dinner companions continued to speculate, Theda took another large gulp of wine. Silent in the sea of chatter, she allowed her senses to stretch through the turbulent ether to the mind of the Mage.

As ever, parsing the mind of her god was heavy going, splintered with distractions and a myriad of different outcomes, like reflections seen in a broken mirror. Maintaining her focus, she waited until the clearest image came to her mind.

The vision he showed her made her jump with fright. Her goblet tumbled from nerveless fingers to spread a stain of red wine like blood over the board. In the distance of her mind, the Mage chuckled like a man about to throw dice, tossing fate in the air with a flick of his fingers. His grim voice tickled her senses, teasing, testing.

"And so the game begins, Theda of the Owls, Seer of Epera. What will you give to save the future?"

Chapter Five

From the journal of Briana of the Owls

The Mage spoke last night. I saw the change in my mother's face. As yet, she will not tell me what she saw. As usual, it will be nothing good. I spoke to the girl they call Ariana of Wessendean. She's friendly enough, for a Citizen, but her dress sense is terrible.

Grateful for the king's absence, the court relaxed as the meal ended and the evening entertainment began. Briana and Ariana were in demand as dance partners. Theda could feel the concern in some members of the Blessed, who were also picking up on the charged atmosphere and talking about it amongst themselves. The Citizens felt nothing amiss, although her sharp ears still caught the rumour as it continued to swirl over the company. Unable to bear the tension and seeking peace from the hailstorm of mental energy, she almost ran the length of the room. She caught Robert Skinner's eye as she hurried out. The look he gave her was grave and perplexed. She understood it completely. It was the same feeling that was buffeting her like a storm wind. Change.

Mind reeling, Theda hurried up the stone stairways. Safe in the sanctuary of her room, she warmed her chilled hands at the fire and wore a pathway across the rug as she paced. She sat for a spell, then jumped up again, unable to relax. Her mind wandered to the queen's chambers where Gwyneth laboured to bring forth her child. Theodora's bland statement about the queen's distress could mean anything from an acute medical emergency to a sudden yearning for out of season fruit.

And yet, and yet...

The anger and doubt she had seen cross the king's face. The jealousy of young Darius. And where was Darius, anyway? Normally, he would be the first on the dance floor, gathering all eyes to him. A mysterious mixture of erudite scholar and worldly glamour.

Her candles burned down to stubs and Theda was lying on her bed, still fully dressed, when the outer door opened and her daughter entered, crackling with nervous energy. Theda propped herself up as Briana lit another candle and took a couple of dance steps, foot fall muffled by the hearthrug, still humming under her breath.

"You had a good evening, Briana?" she called through the half-open door.

Bracing both hands on the doorframe, Briana leaned in, cheeks flushed with wine and exercise. "The Citizens may not do magic, but they know how to dance. And talk."

Theda rubbed her hands over her face to cover a yawn and levered herself to her feet. "That they do," she said, joining her daughter in front of the banked fireplace. "Who did you dance with?"

"An iron merchant from Blade and his nephew. The Montfords. Do you know them?"

"I teach Master Montford's young daughter. He's hunting for a new wife. The last one died in childbirth."

Briana deflated. "Oh."

Despite her concern, Theda chuckled.

"Fear not. There are more eligible partners at the Court of Skies, and not all of them come with ready-made families."

Pouting her irritation, Briana slumped into a chair and massaged her feet. "You think me selfish. Perhaps I am."

"No more so than any other young woman new to court. I would wish you to fall in love. It matters not to me whether your chosen is Blessed."

Briana glanced up, stretching her toes to the warmth of the hearth. "Truly, mother? It would not worry you?"

Theda sighed. "You know as well as I, the Gods bless where they will. Your children could be Blessed, or not, as the Mage wills. Would you love them less if they could not do magic?"

Briana raised her eyebrows. "I hope I would love them equally."

"But many children suffer exactly that fate. Especially here, so close to the king."

"I did hear someone tonight talking about his daughter as if she was a mere servant in his household. A chattel to be rid of. Offloaded to the highest bidder. It is really so bad?"

Theda took the chair opposite her daughter and stared at the dim coals. "At least you noticed. That's something, I suppose."

"That's not fair, mother. I did not ask to be Blessed, nor to the degree that I am."

"All the Mage could ask is that you treat people equally, with the respect they deserve. That is all. It is one reason I wanted you to come. To see how things stand between the Blessed and Citizens first hand."

Briana rose on a yawn and looped slender arms around Theda's neck. "Another one of your interminable lessons?"

Theda placed both hands on her daughter's shoulders and looked at her hard.

"Enough of your blandishments, daughter. Yes, this is a lesson. Perhaps the most important one. Learn it well, child of mine."

"I will, but not tonight. It is late. I am for bed."

Briana dipped a mock curtsey and took her leave. Theda crossed to the window where moonlight painted shadows and silver against the tiltyard walls. A rising wind rippled the pennants in their stands. The Black Eagles of the king's standard flapped their wings against the night. Once again, the prickle of magic in the air tickled the base of her neck, raising the short hairs there. Somewhere outside, the faint hoot of an owl echoed around the ramparts, and she flinched as the bird swooped past, hunting down its prey. She shivered. Owls always represented the presence of the Mage.

Almost in a trance, she abandoned her quiet chamber for the gloomy passageways populated by exhausted servants transporting coal and water for their masters. Intent on their tasks, they took no notice of Theda as she flitted through the shadows, cloak trailing behind her. A faint chime of music still percolated from the distant hall, where late night carousers danced and diced. Frowning, Theda turned away from it, following an inner urging that told her where she had to be. She took another corner and began the precarious descent around the corkscrew stairwell that led to the low-roofed castle kitchens and the service courtyard. The fingers not clutching her cloak trailed cold, greasy stonework, worn smooth with the timeless passage of weary hands.

The kitchens were quiet now, the great fires banked for the night, clanking spits silent, their meals delivered. A memory of supper caressed her nose, along with the less pleasant reek of offal and rotting vegetables from the bins that flanked the outer door, waiting for the kitchen staff to remove to the pig pens and the middens. Huge vats and saucepans hung from hooks suspended from the low ceiling, dull red light reflected on their metal flanks. Theda's footfall disturbed a group of foraging mice and the one of the kitchen cats looked up, black tail swishing, green eyes malevolent. It pounced. Theda winced at the tiny distress call from the unlucky mouse. It's family scattered, terrified. The cat gulped its supper and returned to its place by the fire, licking its whiskers.

Mesmerised by this small drama, Theda jumped when frantic footsteps sounded on the stairwell. She retreated to a shadowed wall as two members of the Queen's household burst into the room.

"We should stay with her, angry as he is..." The head of Gwyneth's household, Floriana of Oceanis, hurried to the fireplace. She bent, reaching for a poker, and gave the coals an experimental prod. The fire flared to obliging life, and Floriana wasted no time hanging a pot of water to heat over the flames, her actions smooth and practiced. Theda waited, as the plump young woman withdrew a small wrap of herbs from her pocket and added it to the water.

"I won't go back. Nor would you if you had any sense. He told us he would look after her." Theodora of Wessendean shivered. "We've surely done enough today."

"She will die if we don't help her. It's been too long. She's too small, and the babe is too big. Find me some honey. This will taste dreadful without it."

"The King can help her. He's powerful. Much more so than us. He will call on the Mage."

Floriana rolled her eyes at the older woman. "The Mage does not understand the ways of women. We need someone from Argentia, blessed by the Empress. They would know what to do." She grabbed an iron spoon and gave the tea a stir. Hidden in the shadows, Theda's nose wrinkled at the pungent herbs that cut through the smell of rancid fat and roasted meat and she gave a silent nod of approval. Black Cohosh and Motherwort tea.

Face screwed into a grimace of resignation, Theodora searched the gloomy kitchen and Theda sighed inwardly when she realised that the vat of honey required to sweeten the bitter taste was right next to her. Relinquishing her cover, she stepped forward into the light of the flames, and the two women jumped out of their skins.

"How dare you! What do you want here?" Theodora advanced, face flushed with heat.

Theda held her gaze. "The honey is here." She tapped the barrel with the tip of her shoe.

"You have no business being down here." Theodora persisted.

"Leave her." Floriana tossed the spoon across the space. Theda caught it, deftly. "This is Mistress Eglion, the Court Librarian. In all likelihood, she knows much more about life in the castle than both of us. Famed for your knowledge. Isn't that right, Mistress?"

Theda avoided the question, dipping the spoon into the vat and conveying it to the steaming pot on the hearth.

"I am at your service, ladies," she said, as she stirred. "Details of the queen's health are safe with me. 'Tis good to know she has such care and concern within her household."

A small smile lifted Floriana's lips as she wrapped her hand in a rag and lifted the iron pot from the flames. Theda handed her a wooden beaker, mind prickling as Theodora's suspicious gaze became a more insistent mental question, seeking entry to her thoughts. She kept her face smooth and stiffened her internal defences. Theodora's Blessed telepathic gift was useful, but not very strong. The curious woman would find nothing of interest in her head apart from a mental image composed entirely of books.

She allowed herself an inward smirk as Theodora withdrew. Sometimes, being dismissed as a mere Citizen was all it took to prevent further intrusion.

Task complete, Floriana nodded to her. "My thanks, Mistress." She turned to Theodora, something more challenging in her gaze. "I am returning to the queen with this. Are you coming?"

"The king won't let you in."

"It is my duty as the queen's friend and companion to try. What about you?"

Theodora heaved a sigh. "You are a braver woman than I will ever be. I will come."

The two women nodded to Theda, who stood back to let them pass. She re-banked the fire, tipped the remains of the tea into the midden bucket.

She had barely reached the first turn of the stair before the kitchen cat killed another mouse.

Chapter Six

From the journal of Briana of the Owls, Court of the Skies, Castle of Air

Lord Darius of Falconridge is the most interesting man here. He dances like a dream, and I get to see him every day in the Great Library, which has to be the most boring place the Gods ever saw. He's charming, but very remote. Ariana says he's enjoying his new position but is not interested in taking a bride. I wonder if I can get him to change his mind?

Dreams punctuated with nightmares and a chilly spring gale that rattled through the gaps between pane and glass saw Theda rise with the dawn to scurry back to the kitchen courtyard for wood and coal. Untidy servants, already sweating under their hoods, yawning like her, nodded to her as she passed. She'd left Briana abed, curls tumbled across her thin pillow, a light frown creasing her unlined brow.

Pulling her cloak more securely around her, Theda shivered in the breeze that bellied around the outer yard. The sun peeped across the mountains, turning the sky to amber, but patches of black ice lurked beneath the shadowed walls, outside the coal shed, ready to trick the unwary. She transferred her iron bucket to her other hand, blowing on her chilled fingers before stooping for a shovel. The clang of coal as she loaded up echoed around the castle walls.

Bucket full, she gritted her teeth and heaved it upward as the ground appeared to shake beneath her. The starlings flew shrieking from the battlements into the crisp morning air. Taken by surprise and unbalanced by the load, she uttered a small cry of alarm as her foot skidded and she hit the ground with a smack that jarred her shoulder and sent a shock wave of pain through her left knee. The bucket turned on the ice like a skater across a winter pond, spraying its contents across the rough flags, and a wave of dizziness engulfed her.

Swearing under her breath as the courtyard walls whirled, Theda sat for a moment, rubbing her leg. Something had happened. She still felt the ground trembling beneath her. Scared. As if something had attacked it. Was it an earthquake? Her puzzled gaze followed the flight of the starlings as they swirled in angry circles, unwilling to land.

"Mistress, are you well? Did you hit your head?"

The sturdy young man standing in front of her wore the uniform of the castle guard. Dark blue trimmed with silver. A standard issue sword in a battered leather scabbard lay against his left hip and his boots were wet. Theda had a good view of them from her position on the floor, where the damp permeated her clothing.

The soldier leaned down, offering his arm. His cloak smelled of tobacco and spices. Theda allowed herself to be hauled to her feet, wincing at the pain in her knee. "Did you feel that?" she asked him, bending to rub her leg.

"Feel what?"

"The ground shook. Surely you felt it?"

Her rescuer gave her a puzzled look. "Are you sure you didn't hit your head? You should be more careful," he chided, righting the bucket and busying himself collecting her spilled coal. Still somewhat dazed by the unexpected fall, she reached for the replenished load. The soldier shook his head, dark eyes laughing, and offered her his elbow.

"I will see you and your bucket to your chamber, Mistress. Jacklyn Sommerton, at your service."

"I thank you." She threw one last look at the scared castle starlings as Jacklyn helped her across the watchful courtyard and shivered as a cloud crossed the morning sun.

Grateful for the help, Theda lurched behind her new escort through the busy kitchens. Jacklyn exchanged cheerful comments with the cooks and kitchen maids they passed, snatching a hot loaf of bread and a hunk of cheese on his way through. He dodged a smack around the head with a laugh that started somewhere in his belly. Smiles followed him. Jacklyn waved his loaf at the nearest servers in salute. He tore the bread in half, releasing a cloud of steam. Placing half a portion carefully in a small knapsack hung from his shoulder, he handed her the rest, along with a piece of cheese.

"Here. Breakfast. Where are you lodged?"

Theda told him. Jacklyn nodded, striding along with all the confidence of healthy youth. "Citizen or Blessed?" he asked, conversationally, as they reached the Gallery, a wide, many windowed thoroughfare that demarcated the public rooms of the castle from the living quarters.

"Citizen. Mistress Theda Eglion, Librarian." she said.

Jacklyn glanced down at her, amused. "Ah. I never had much use for book learning," he said. "Not much used to heaving heavy buckets around then."

Theda dipped her head, acknowledging his point. “Books, yes. Buckets no.” she said.

“And you’ve no servants, or husband or suitor to do for you?”

“Clearly not.”

“I’ll do it. Every morning. And welcome.”

They had reached the one of the wider stairways that climbed the levels of the castle. Heavy portraits in gilded frames painted in the old style hung from the walls. A gallery of long dead kings and queens, pale and tall.

“You don’t have....” Theda began, but Jacklyn had forged ahead, his long legs taking the steep treads two at a time, already near the second floor. Her knee throbbing, Theda leaned on the stone balustrade to aid her ascent.

Head buzzing, she slowed to a halt on the first landing, conscious of the nearest servants flattening themselves into invisibility against the walls of the torch lit corridor. Theda blinked. Only one person at Court had that effect, and it wasn’t her. Following their lead, she pressed herself against the stone wall on the landing, under the cautious, thoughtful gaze of an ancient queen.

King Francis strode the length of the passageway, staring ahead at nothing, face fixed and pale with grief. Eyes wide, Theda’s horrified gaze dropped to the tiny, blanket wrapped form he held in his arms. She clamped a hand to her mouth to smother her gasp of dismay, heart crushed with pity and pain.

Unbidden, her mind reached for the King’s. As a telepath, like her, his thoughts were usually clear to see, unless he was defending them, but there was nothing there that she could read. Frowning, she pushed a little harder, probing through the blank mask of shock. Still nothing.

King Francis moved like a man in a dream. Heads revolved in his wake, marking his departure down the magnificent stone stairs to the gallery. The tiny body in his arms did not stir. Theda saw a single tear on the king's cheek, glinting in the light of the nearest torch as he passed her by in a rustle of dark blue velvet.

Cheeks frozen with disbelief, she watched as the king retreated, back stiff and straight. Forbidding. The servants returned her alarmed expression, muttering amongst themselves as they retrieved their burdens and continued their tasks. Wrapping her cloak around her, heart heavy, Theda continued her halting journey. Hauling herself up the last stair, her eyes jerked up at the sound of a distant scream coming from the Queen's suite in the South wing.

She stopped in her tracks, swaying against the wall as the scream sounded again and somehow she knew.

The Queen was dead.

Chapter Seven

From the journal of Briana of the Owls

Everyone is devastated with the news about the Queen. It's very sad, her and her baby too. Ariana says she suffered dreadfully giving birth. Is it always that way for us? What will happen to me when I have children?

Over the next few days, word of the queen's death shot through the castle, around the kingdom and across the wider continent as though fired from a cannon.

Rudderless without their rulers, the Court of Skies huddled in small, bewildered groups. Gossip was rife. Grim faced later in the morning, Theda and Briana took a turn around the castle gallery, where Ariana confirmed what Theda had discovered a few hours before. The queen had died in childbirth, after a long and gruelling labour that resulted in the death of her child. A boy. The king had tried everything he knew to save her. It had not been enough.

Lord Peterson, the Chamberlain, ordered the court to mourn in black. The king kept to his rooms, where his grief seemed somehow to leach through his locked door and into the minds of his people. Even the birds wheeling at their tasks in the watchful sky appeared to do so in shocked silence.

The ladies of her household transported Gwyneth to the chapel to lie in state and took turns to watch over her coffin. Eyes swollen with tears, nobility, the Blessed, Citizens, and servants alike took some time to watch with them. Gwyneth had been gentle, revered, respected. Without her, the court showed a harder face. Less forbearing. Less kind. Priests and priestesses of the Mage lit candles. Early spring flowers lay as offerings in shrines and temples throughout Epera. Meals took place as usual. People drank more, and Girdred played plaintiff ballads, his soft, bearded face distant as he wet the strings of his harp with his tears. On the day of her funeral, the combined clergy of Epera and Oceanis, along with King Merlon and Queen Clarys, laid Gwyneth to rest in the Eagle's catacombs that stretched beneath the castle chapel. King Francis stared into space as the priests sealed the entrance, his face severe. He looked smaller somehow, stubble-lined cheeks shrunken, shoulders stooped. Despite her subtle efforts, Theda still found it impossible to penetrate his thoughts.

Taking her place at her desk in the Great Library on the morning that lessons resumed ten long days later, Theda marvelled at the change in atmosphere. Grey cloud swallowed the spring sunlight, and the dull light did little to illuminate her work. Robert Skinner rose to light the lamps early in the morning, and they burned on throughout the day. Scholars studied in virtual silence. Some simply stared into space, tears standing in their eyes.

At midday, stomach growling, Theda cast an irritated glance at the line of trolleys laden with study material, waiting to be returned to the shelves. Briana had disappeared into the stacks with one of them earlier in the morning, but she was not as quick as the experienced Darius, and the resulting log jam was affecting the smooth processing of loans.

Briana began a slow return from the mathematics section, dragging her empty trolley behind like a reluctant toddler. Someone growled at her as it bumped against their desk and she snapped back, hands on hips. Theda abandoned her work to smooth the situation before her daughter's hasty words and temper started a riot.

"Let me take that for you, child," she said as she neared. "The trolleys are harder to control when they are empty." She telegraphed a warning glare to her offspring and nodded towards the sanctuary of her desk. Briana gave up the cold iron handle and marched away, shoulders tense.

"I hate shelving books. It's the most boring thing I've ever done in my life," Briana hissed as Theda approached, parked the trolley, and started sorting the contents of its neighbour into order.

Theda quelled her with one long, quiet look and nodded at one of the other trolleys. "It is a job that needs to be done. It will be quicker with two." Her eyes and fingers moved swiftly across the titles, organising them by subject and author.

"Where's Darius, anyway? Isn't this his job?" Briana yanked at the cover of a book and forced it into another position.

Theda frowned, her eyes still on her work. "I don't know," she said. "I've hardly seen him since..."

"But he is here. I saw him this morning. He's right at the back." Briana jerked her hand behind her, and Theda straightened.

"At the back? In the Restricted section? How did he get in there? You didn't..."

Briana bit her lip, scarlet flooding her cheeks as she realised her mistake. She looked at the floor. "I gave him the key."

Theda's hands stopped. Blood drained from her cheeks. She stared at Briana in disbelief.

"You gave Darius, a Citizen, the key to the Restricted section that houses the most potentially dangerous magical works in the entire continent?"

Theda did not raise her voice, but Briana cringed at her words.

"I'm sorry," she mumbled, fists clenched. "I didn't realise."

"I told you on your very first day here. No-one goes in the Restricted section unless I accompany them."

"He said he'd only be a minute. He said he was fetching something for you."

"And he's been there four hours. You stay here. Mind the desk. If I am not back when they call us for our meal, send for the guard."

Face a grim mask, Theda whirled, grabbed a lantern and set off down the room, robes swirling dust from the floor. Darius, with his retentive memory, and mercurial nature, let loose in her precious magical collection. She'd think twice before letting Robert Skinner in there, let alone a Citizen.

Far from the warmth of the massive fireplace, the shelves at the far end of the library always loomed chill and watchful. Theda clutched her cloak more securely around her, her eyes darting left and right, hoping to see the feather of Darius's hat bent over a title in a place other than where he was not supposed to be.

Professor Theodor of Gossington raised his greying, jowly beard at her in the economics section, but apart from him, this end of the library lay quiet and abandoned. Jaw clenched, Theda took in the heavy, ornate door with its delicate scroll work carved with the sign of the Mage that housed the magical collection. Lantern light gilded its edges. Her feet made no sound as she reached it and pushed it open.

Searching for misplaced items, Theda's eyes flicked around the space. Epera's collection of magical works crammed every shelf of the stone walled room. Scrolls nearly a thousand years old, shelved in glass cases bound with iron facings, stood in a long line at the centre. Wooden boxes housed precious artefacts, inventions and gadgets, the projects of a thousand years of Epera's magical experimentation. Ancient, delicate manuscripts contained treatises on the workings of the mind, the ways of the Mage, the differences between the Blessed of the four nations of Altius Mysterium. Prayers, charms, spells, hand gestures, meditations. Essays and diagrams. All here. The most important collection of magical works on the entire continent. Even the dry air contained within its walls prickled her magical senses and floated the hairs on her arms. There was a gap on one of the crowded shelves. As obvious as a missing tooth.

"You should not be in here."

Her voice sounded overloud in the confined space. Almost lost in the shadows, Darius spun around, clutching his prize with covetous hands that, to Theda's charged mind, suddenly appeared more like claws.

His chin lifted. "Briana gave me a key."

"She made a mistake." Holding out her hand, Theda took a couple of paces towards him, conscious of his height and the knife at his belt. She frowned. Jaw locked with tension, black eyes expressionless, the young man held her gaze. She shook her head. There was something wrong here. The youthful library assistant, so eager to help, appeared to be absent, replaced by a stranger. There was something else missing as well.

His smile.

"Darius." Somehow, she injected authority into her tone, despite the acceleration in her heartbeat and her alarm at his silent, wary presence. "Give me the key. And that book. This is no place for you."

His chin jerked as if she had hit him. His black eyes narrowed to slits. "Then nor you, Mistress." he said, raising one eyebrow. "A mere Citizen, like myself."

"A Citizen charged to protect Epera's knowledge. All of it. Including this section. You know the rules."

The edges of his famous smile curved his lips. "But I have the key." He dug in the pocket of his jerkin and held it out to her, iron thick and dark with the patina of time. It twisted on its blue ribbon like an unknowable fate presenting first one side, and then the other.

Theda stiffened. There would be little she could do against his strength should he refuse to hand it over. She dared not compel him using magic.

"I will tell you only once more, and then it will be the guard and the King you will answer to."

To her surprise, he chuckled. The sound was cruel, with little humour in it. "The King is not of sound mind," he said. "I doubt the man knows the day of the week."

"He is mourning the loss of his wife and child. It is no wonder. The key and the book, if you please." She held her hand out once more, willing her fingers not to tremble.

Darius's lips twisted and for one terrible second, she thought he would refuse, but then he shrugged and took a step forward, dropping the disputed items into her waiting palm.

"'Tis of no matter. I have what I came for. Your servant, Mistress." He said, sketching her a mocking bow.

She stepped back, clearing a path to the door as he sauntered past, trailing his fingers in an almost lustful caress across the lines of books.

She shivered at his action, a frown screwed across her forehead. The eager boy of the past few years had disappeared. This glib, impudent stranger, was someone else. Someone she could no longer trust.

"Darius." she called after him, as he crossed the threshold.

He waited, tension in every line of him, but did not do her the honour of turning about. In the end, she spoke to his velvet clad back.

"I will no longer require your services in the library. From now on, I revoke your right to browse at your leisure. In the future, should you wish to borrow an item, you will tell me, and I will see it retrieved for you. Do you understand?"

She waited for a response, but he still refused to face her. His head jerked an acknowledgement before he strode away. Theda strung the precious key securely around her neck. No longer would it reside in the top drawer of her desk. Her eyes dropped to the book Darius had been perusing with such interest, and another frown darkened her brow.

"Ye Aspects of ye Gods." by Professor Winterhorne. Pursing her lips, she flicked through the contents. It was a dry tome, highlighting the Great Gods in their various presentations. She couldn't imagine how it would benefit a Citizen like Darius. She gave the volume a pat before returning it to its shelf and indulged herself with another fond look at her collection. Loose pages fluttered as her gaze passed across them. The heavier items rocked in place in greeting. Theda put her finger to her lips and smiled at her charges.

"Ssh," she said. "Remember, you are in a library."

Chapter Eight

From the journal of Briana of the Owls.

I knew it wouldn't be long before I did something wrong. Apparently, I should not have given the key to the Restricted section to Darius, even though he studies everything and actually works here. But he smiled at me and promised me a dance if I would. A dance with Darius! It was worth my mother's anger, just for that.

Hurrying back to her cluttered desk as the lunchtime exodus began, Theda fixed her daughter with a glare that should have burned her to ashes where she stood. Briana's eyes widened when she saw the banked rage there, and she withered beneath it, placing her quill carefully aside, cheeks scarlet.

"Come. We are late."

Theda swept past Briana into the chilly, lamplit passageway and barrelled through the crowd like a storm, leaving the girl to scurry in her wake.

"What is it? What's the matter?"

"Young Darius is the matter, that's what. You have just lost me the best library assistant I have ever had. I cannot believe all the lad had to do was smile, and you melted."

"Why have you lost him? That was not of my doing." Annoyingly, Briana kept pace with her. Theda shook off her restraining arm.

"He had taken a book from the Restricted section. Didn't want to give it back." Theda stopped suddenly, and dragged Briana to the wall, away from the hungry throng of people heading for the Great Hall on a tide of chatter.

"I can't let him continue to have a free rein, Briana. In the future, we will treat him as a borrower and scholar, like all the rest. He will not wander the stacks at will. I will request a guard to be placed if I have to."

"That is a little harsh, don't you think?"

Theda sighed. "I can't explain it. The lad has grown up overnight. Just a few short days ago, he was biddable, compliant. Now..." she shook her head. "For a moment, I feared him, Briana. I really did."

Briana snorted and took her arm, dragging her back into the crowd. "He's just a boy. A simple Citizen. He can't do us any harm. Not really."

"I'd rather you had nothing to do with him."

"Ah..."

"What now?"

Briana looked at her feet. "Well, I did promise him a dance tonight. Or two."

Theda stopped and put her hands on her hips, stumbling slightly as a hurrying noble crashed into her from behind. She ignored his angry protest. "Was this before, or after, you gave him that gods damned key?"

"Um, well actually... before."

Theda barked a laugh and shook her head. Darius may be young, but his strategy was perfect. "Oh, my girl. You have such a lot to learn."

"You can't tell me how to run my life, mother." Head in the air, Briana marched away. Theda huffed a sigh that issued from the depths of her being, and started when a familiar, masculine hand slid under her elbow to propel her forward.

"Come, Mistress," Robert Skinner said, briskly. "I am for dinner. You look like you lost a sixpence and found a farthing."

"Something like that," Theda admitted, grateful for his concern.

"Another young maiden smitten by Lord Falconridge?"

Theda's lips thinned. "So it seems."

Robert laughed. "Not such a poor match, Mistress."

She shivered as her blood chilled.

"I wouldn't say that, Robert."

"Why ever not? Darius of Falconridge, rich, titled, studious, charming. A Citizen, I know, but surely there could be no better match for her?"

"On the surface, a good match, to be sure. Although I have had to dismiss him as my assistant this morning."

Robert glanced at her with a question in his eyes, and Theda shared the events of the morning with him as they took their places for lunch. Briana pointedly removed herself from her mother's company and took a bench with Ariana a few spaces below Darius and his cronies. Their laughter grated on her ears above the hum of chatter.

"Do you know what he was looking at?" Robert asked her, at the end of her tale.

"*Ye Aspects of Ye Gods*" by Professor Winterhorne. You'll know of it. A simple discussion of the Gods and their two faces. He appeared mesmerised by it as I entered, but I can't think why." Her voice trailed off as she considered the ramifications.

"Perhaps this is a conversation best kept private, Mistress?"

Theda jumped as Robert's mental voice penetrated her thoughts. Her eyes snapped to his.

"Ah, I thought it must be so. Only a member of the Blessed could discuss the contents of a book from the Restricted section." Robert tipped his goblet at her and regarded her steadily over the rim as he raised it to his lips, one eyebrow raised.

Kicking herself for being drawn so easily into conversation, Theda avoided his questioning stare and looked at the thick mess of pottage in the bowl in front of her. Steam rose from its contents, and she clamped a hand over her mouth against the urge to be sick. How could she let him into her mind so easily, after all she had warned Briana on the subject?

Robert squeezed her arm. *"Do not be concerned, Mistress, or may I call you Theda? If you wish your gifts to remain hidden, 'tis your business and no-one shall know from my lips."*

Her fingers shook as she picked up her spoon and stirred the stew, focusing on the circular motion as she brought her breathing under control. The din of conversation dulled as she concentrated her mental energy on balancing her magical gift, blocking her own thoughts and enhancing the mental voices of those Blessed with telepathy. Advanced and powerful, Robert's voice sounded loud in her head, his mental chat as open and friendly as usual. Briana, sitting a few seats away, kept a heavy cloak on her thoughts. There were fewer Blessed with telepathy at court than she had once thought. Theodora of Wessendean's gift was small. There was the usual blank from the Citizens, huddled at their bowls. Two other tutors were deep in a telepathic conversation at the other side of the room. She wondered which of them might have been thinking about the paternity of the queen's child on the night prior to her death. Her gaze flicked up. Clarissa Weston and Cerys

O'Neil sisters from Goldfern, near the border with Oceanis. Both inveterate gossips, although excellent teachers. She supposed either of them could be responsible.

Brow contracting, her narrowed stare carried on around the ranks of the courtiers. Here and there amongst the servants, a latent gift yet to be trained. At the top table, King Francis propped his bearded chin on his hand and kept his eyes fixed on his plate. The empty seat beside him was a dreadful reminder of his loss. Her eyes crept back to him. Still nothing. Was he blocking? On his right, Lord Chancellor, Sir Walter Smythe, another powerful member of the Blessed at the Court of Skies had his small, close-set eyes fixed on the rowdy bunch of Citizens around Darius. She could follow the train of his thoughts easily. *"Too big for their britches, that little lot. About time someone put that lad Darius in his place,"*

She sighed. There was no point in keeping Robert out of her thoughts now. There were too many questions in her mind that demanded discussion, if not answers.

"I am worried about the King," she said. *"I cannot hear him at all."*

"Yes, I noticed that as well. He has been quiet since the death of dear Gwyneth."

"I suppose that might be shock, or grief, but I would think either of those may open his mind, rather than cause him to close it."

"But he is the King. He has always had incredible control."

"He looks ill."

"I heard he is not eating."

Theda spooned a portion of stew into her mouth. Despite appearances, the rich vegetables and floury potatoes warmed her tight stomach. She glanced over to the top table again, where the King was talking to Theodora across the empty chair between them. Theodora must have managed some sort of miracle, because a smile lightened the old king's face by a small degree, and he patted her hand.

"Then let us hope he comes back to us soon. The country will need an heir," she said.

"A new wife." Robert's speculative gaze drifted up the table to where Briana bantered with the group of young men around Darius. Briana had pulled their pack of playing cards towards her and begun a rowdy game of Taroc. The space in front of them was a littered mess of empty bowls, half full goblets and small piles of coins.

Theda removed her spoon from her bowl and batted it sharply on the back of his hand. Robert flinched.

"Not Briana," she said.

Despite the careful block Theda was keeping on their conversation, some of it must have leaked to her daughter.

Jaw tight, Briana glanced round, pale cheeks flushed with wine, grey eyes glittering. Theda raised one eyebrow. Briana tossed her head and returned to her companions. Her mother could only watch as she nudged Darius' sleeve to get his attention and raised the stakes in the game. Darius replied something that caused the entire group to rock with laughter, loud in the subdued atmosphere.

Alerted by the commotion, Francis stiffened in his chair and murmured to the servant who waited behind him. The man nodded briskly and made his way across to the rowdy table. Theda and Robert exchanged alarmed glances when Darius left his place to approach his monarch. A low murmur of conversation followed in his wake. Francis rarely required the attention of a Citizen. Darius made his way to the royal dais with casual grace, his cold, pale face a mask of dutiful compliance. He swept Francis a bow and leaned closer to hear what the King had to say. Alert for new gossip, the courtiers dropped all pretence of not listening. The room hushed. Spoons ceased to scrape. Tankards lowered.

"You know we do not permit gambling at the noonday meal," Francis said. Cracked with disuse, his voice was much quieter than before the queen's death.

Lips thinning, Theda darted a narrow glance at Briana, whose cheeks flushed further with mortification. She would not have known. And none of her group had attempted to dissuade her when she grabbed the deck of cards.

"Your pardon, my lord," Darius's voice echoed clear to the rafters. "We were playing for pennies to donate to the poor."

"Indeed. And whose idea was that?"

Silence. Theda held her breath and started when Robert gripped the hand she had clenched around the fabric of her skirt under the table. Darius opened his mouth to speak, but Briana was faster. Brushing aside Ariana's restraining arm, she swung her long legs over the bench and made her way up the narrow aisle between the crowded tables to join him. Theda's heart thumped in her chest as her daughter dipped into a court curtsey that would have graced a princess. Darius surveyed her with one eyebrow raised. Briana did not look at him.

"It was my idea, Your Majesty. I am new to court, and was not aware of the rules. My apologies."

Francis took his time in looking her up and down. "And you are?" he questioned, raising a glass of wine to his lips.

Briana paused before she answered, and Theda's fingers twisted within Robert's warm clasp. "Briana Eglion, Citizen of Epera."

Theda let out her breath in a rush, and Robert squeezed her hand. "*T'will be alright. She will not give you away.*"

"Eglion, you say?" Francis frowned. "Any relation to...?"

"Mistress Eglion, Your Majesty."

"Ah, of course, our celebrated scholar and librarian." Francis lifted his gaze, scanning the ranks of his people, and Theda sighed. Uncomfortable under the avid gaze of the court, she missed the comforting warmth of Robert's hand as she hurried to join the small group in front of the throne. Dropping into a deep curtsey as she drew level, Theda had her first good look at the King since the death of the queen. There was little comfort in his tired face. Blue eyes that had once crackled with energy and intelligence now held all the remorse of a chastised hound. He appeared smaller somehow, dwarfed by the expanse of ermine and velvet that swamped his slender frame. His famous ring hung slack and dull on the forefinger of his right hand.

"Your daughter is welcome to our court, Mistress, and her beauty and grace are much admired... but school her on the customs and observances at mealtimes," he said.

"Yes, your Majesty." Theda shot a meaningful glance at Briana, who dipped into another obedient curtsey for good measure.

"Lord Darius, I have heard much of your scholarship in recent months, and I find a vacancy has arisen in my service as a Clerk. Mind you to take it?"

There was a long silence. Theda risked a glance at her former assistant's face, where Darius appeared to be struggling to control his expression. Surely, the correct response was to agree. After all, the lad was out of a useful occupation since this morning, and service to the King was a road to further advancement. Why would he not jump at the honour?

She watched as Darius swallowed past the tension in his jaw, and his smooth cheeks flushed with what should be pleasure but looked more like rage. He bowed.

"You honour me, your Majesty."

"Then report to the Lord Chamberlain after the meal. He will instruct you further." The King nodded in dismissal, and the group withdrew to their places as the reanimated courtiers turned to each other with fresh gossip on their lips. Theda took her place next to Robert and stared numbly at the tankard of pale ale Robert pulled towards her with a slight gesture of his fingers. Briana threw her a look of haughty triumph as she returned to her friends. Theda's heart sank along with her drink when Darius turned the charm of his smile on her daughter. Briana's cheeks pinked as she collected the playing cards and stacked them carefully before she handed them back.

"I dislike where this is going," Theda said, raising the drink to suddenly dry lips.

"Francis does your daughter great honour in commending her in front of the court. She will not lack for offers after this. I see the Count of Dupliss is already smitten with her, as is Master Pemberton from Swan's Reach. Look."

Her companion nudged her arm to draw her attention. Theda glanced around at the courtiers he had mentioned. Robert saw the situation true. Only a couple of weeks at court and Briana had already gathered a flock of potential suitors. They eyed her with interest, some more lustful than others, and Theda shivered as a draft crossed her slim shoulders under her cloak.

Her eyes centred on Briana once more. The young girl's face was upturned towards Darius. Open and bright like a flower to the sun.

"T'is not the men who are interested in Briana that concern me," she said, hiding her grim expression in her cup. *"T'is who Briana has set her sights upon that bothers me most."*

Chapter Nine

From the diary of Briana of the Owls

Darius lied to the king for me! Of course, we were not gambling for pennies to feed the poor, we were just having fun. That has to mean something! I don't care what my mother says, or even if he is just a Citizen. He must care about me a little, and I still see him in the library most days. Despite my mother's restrictions, he can't seem to stay away.

Despite forbidding Darius free access to the library shelves, Theda found him requesting more and more titles as the season turned from spring to summer, and he buried himself in tasks for his new employer, the King.

Happy to oblige, Briana would leave her work to accompany him, and Theda could only huff a sigh as the two disappeared into the stacks. Briana was of age, and the dark-faced stranger she had confronted weeks ago seemed to have receded, replaced by the more cheerful and charming youth of her first acquaintance. She missed his work ethic. Briana had not settled well into her magic-free labour in the library. In the end, Theda pressed Robert Skinner's son, Terrence, into service to shelve the books. Broad-shouldered and happy to oblige, Terrence had no trouble taming the heavy, recalcitrant trolleys, leaving Briana the more favoured task of tending the desk. When not studying or working, he followed Briana with round, puppy-dog eyes, enduring his father's good-humoured barrage of teasing with few complaints. Wrapped up in her budding romance with Darius, Briana barely noticed him, although Theda could wish the situation otherwise. Adding to her puzzlement, the King did not seem to improve as time went on. His telepathy had not returned. He had not regained the weight he had lost. Darius appeared to ride high in the King's esteem. Somehow, the young man had earned himself a place on the top table and the title of King's Secretary, a position of great recognition. His status was assured when the King granted him permission to enter the Grand Tournament. No longer did people call him "the lad, Darius". The Blessed and Citizens now referred to him as "My Lord of Falconridge." Proximity to the King carried its own reward.

"*Mines and Mining* again?" Theda asked as he handed her another pile of books to be checked out one pale, late-summer morning.

Darius shrugged, his smile firmly in place. "His Majesty wishes us to increase our output from the Iron Mountains," he said. "We are to concentrate our efforts on the manufacture of metal goods in the future."

Theda raised her brows. "Where will you find more miners?" she asked. "It is not the most pleasant of occupations, after all."

"You need not bother yourself with that, Mistress. The King and I have a plan for it." He nodded at her and left the desk with the pile of heavy books tucked under his arm. Theda watched him go with her hands on her hips. He'd broadened out in recent months. Mooning over Darius had become one of Briana's favourite pastimes since Darius had entered the Grand Tournament. Normally out of bounds for Citizens, Darius had taken on one opponent after the next in all the games and competitions it contained, from hawking to tennis to swordplay and chess. He contested with all the zeal of a hardened warrior. The youth had become a man. Favourite of the King.

All eyes were on Darius again later in the week when the court gathered at the indoor tennis court on the eastern side of the castle for the last match of the Grand Tournament. Viewing galleries surrounded the court on all sides, and members of the Court of Skies vied for places on the front rows where they could see all the action. Unlike the strict rules concerning gambling at dinner, no such restriction applied to sports. The Blessed and Citizens alike raced to place their bets as Darius, and his opponent, the tall, elegant Lord Chancellor, Sir Walter Smythe from Hallows Gulf, warmed up. Both men's faces were already tight with concentration as they jogged in place and rotated their shoulders under thin cambric shirts. Tying for first place in the Grand Tournament so far, they played for a purse of gold coins, but more than that, the winner would earn the King's preferment, a prize worth having indeed. The court was in a flutter, anticipating the feast to be held later in the evening when the King would announce his decision. The prize could be whatever the King chose. Former champions had received anything from a grant from the privy purse to a prestigious council appointment to property and land.

"What do you think, mother? Will Darius win? Should we place a bet?" Eyes alight with excitement, Briana shook her leather purse, where a few coins jingled. In keeping with their supposed income, she had conjured a modest outfit of emerald green. Slim fitting and elegant, it contrasted well with her dark red curls. She stood on tiptoe, straining to see over the shoulders of Count Dupliss, another fine player, who had commandeered a choice position over the court and readied himself to referee. Theda rolled her eyes. Packed beside Briana and Ariana in the crowded Citizens gallery, her shoulders contracted with tension. Perspiration gathered under her armpits, and she wished she had foregone her favourite serge cloak. The mood was febrile. Almost as if the avid crowd spoiled for a fight. Glares and icy looks darted across the court from the Citizens to the Blessed, lined up in their own observation gallery. She frowned. The change in atmosphere had grown over the summer. Battle lines drawn up between Citizen and Blessed.

Someway behind them, Robert Skinner, a man well regarded for his quick wits and honesty, acted as master of the wagers. "Odds on Sir Walter, ten to one," he chanted. "Place your bets!"

"I'm placing a gold sovereign on the King's favourite, when he chooses," Ariana announced, bracing herself on the rail and peering over. "Oh look, the King is on his way."

The buzz of the crowd hushed briefly for the blast of trumpets and obeisance that announced the King's arrival. He entered the high-walled tennis court through a door at the side and approached the drooping net. The two opponents bowed, and the court waited for the royal approval. In the past, the queen had performed this honour, but now Francis carried out the expected ritual himself. Stooped in his furs, he looked from one man to the other, fingering a gauze scarf in midnight blue as he decided. Theda read Sir Walter's mind with ease, and his casual stance telegraphed his confidence in the King's decision. The man fully expected the scarf to drop on his side of the net. After all, he was a member of the Blessed. And everyone knew what Francis felt about the Citizens and their lack of magical ability. Pack animals, fit for the most rudimentary of tasks and nothing else. A murmur of confusion arose all around Theda as the time dragged out. What was taking Francis so long?

A gasp of shock swept every gallery around the court when Francis dropped the scarf on the ground on Darius's side of the net.

Ariana squealed with excitement and squeezed through the crowd to place her bet with Robert. Briana and Theda exchanged glances. Briana's face blushed with happiness, her grey eyes alight. "The King favours Darius!" she breathed, clutching her hands together.

"Yes, who would have thought it?" Theda replied dryly, mind racing.

Darius's normally pale face flushed with triumph as he bowed to the King and bent to pick up the strip of gauze and tie it to his arm. His dark eyes glinted with malicious light as he squared off with Sir Walter, who looked for a second utterly dumbfounded and gaped at his monarch like a landed fish. Francis carefully ignored his frantic gaze as he left the court for his seat in the gallery, where Theodora of Wessendean waited with a glass of wine. The two had become close companions of late. So much so that gossip had placed bets on Theodora becoming the next Queen of Epera.

"Shall we play?" Darius asked, twisting his wooden racket in both hands. His voice rang around the walls.

Sir Walter's face screwed in a scowl as he scooped a ball from the floor and tossed it experimentally in one broad palm. "You young pup. You may have the King's favour, but you have to get past me for the purse."

"I have no need for the purse." Darius stretched his shoulders.

"Just the preferment. Careful where your ambition takes you, lad. There is a long road ahead and many a slip for the unwary."

Darius shrugged. "We tread the same path, my lord. Take your own warning."

Glaring at each other over the net, the two men took their positions. A blast from Dupliss's wooden whistle, and the game began.

An hour later, plastered with sweat and with the crowd in raptures at the standard of play, the opponents were so evenly matched, no one could predict the outcome. Even King Francis, roused from his self-absorption, leaned against the gallery on the opposite side of the court to cheer them on. Briana and Ariana had their arms around each other and added their shouts along with the rest of the court.

Nerves jangling, Theda slipped away to where Robert was still busy with people wanting to alter their bets. "Evens," he said to one disgruntled noble as she approached. "It's evens."

He raised a harassed gaze to her as she joined him. "Even the Blessed want to change their minds," he grumbled.

"What do you make of it?"

"The match or the King's favour?"

Theda raised a brow. "Which do you think?"

Robert huffed a laugh and shuffled the betting slips into a neater pile. *'T'is clear the Citizens are having a moment in the sun,"* he admitted, as the chant of 'Darius, Darius' bounced around the gallery along with the tennis ball, to meet cries of "Walter, Walter!" coming back the other way.

Theda inclined her head. *"Yes, but why?"* she continued mentally. "*After all this time and everything we know about King Francis and his disdain for Citizens?"*

Robert's face clouded as he considered the question. *"Young Darius is charming company when he wants to be,"* he offered.

"Enough to charm a man as experienced as the King? I don't think so."

"Tournament point. Quiet, please!" Dupliss yelled over the hubbub.

Robert straightened from his task as the cheers from the audience hushed. After the din of the last hour, the tense silence was striking.

"So then, Darius has something the King needs. Something he cannot get for himself."

The two old friends exchanged glances. The clatter of the last serve was almost lost amid the clapping, whistles, and cheers of the Citizens as Darius won the match. On the King's side of the gallery, the Blessed stared at each other, as silent as stones.

Robert had time for one last thought before a tide of jubilant Citizens rushing to claim their winnings overwhelmed him.

"What do we pride ourselves on most in Epera?"

Theda didn't need to think about it.

"Knowledge," she said.

"Will you calm down?" Theda demanded several hours later when she and Briana returned to their room to dress for the feast. "You will make yourself ill, spending so much magic at once."

Thanks to Jacklyn, who, true to his promise, kept them well supplied with coal, their small quarters glowed in the light of the flames. The resultant heat enabled them to stand comfortably in their undergarments to peruse the contents of their cedarwood chests for suitable outfits. Or at least, Theda was turning out the contents of her chest, laying the few robes and sleeves she had on her bed to consider. She pulled her last sleeve from beneath the worn cover of her book of shadows, and regarded it with her head on one side, smoothing out the creases. Briana stood in front of the fire, conjuring robe after robe as her imagination saw fit. Theda shook her head as her daughter brushed her hands down her body, and something silky in midnight blue took the place of the yellow satin trimmed with lace that had comprised the previous attempt.

"Remember who we are supposed to be," Theda said, placing her normal, everyday wool aside and brushing the nap of her favourite blue velvet. "You are conjuring outfits fit for a queen, and we are anything but royalty."

Briana pursed her lips, turning this way and that in front of a full-length mirror that she had conjured to aid her efforts. "Ariana is wearing green tonight. So I can't. It's a pity. Green really does not suit her." She waved her hand again. Amethyst purple trimmed with creamy lace at the neck and sleeves appeared. Theda nodded her approval.

"Yes, that will do. Simple and not too obvious. It looks like something you could have brought with you."

Briana turned in front of her mirror. "It's a bit plain."

"It's elegant. Help me with my sleeves."

Briana left her purple as it was and hurried over. "Black sleeves or blue?" she asked, reaching for the dish of pins.

"Blue, I think."

"You should really let me conjure you something. The nap on this velvet is wearing thin." Briana worked swiftly, fixing the sleeves of Theda's worn court gown to the bodice, careful not to prick her.

Theda huffed a laugh. "What, and risk you forgetting to keep your concentration on my illusion and your own? One look at young Darius and you would have me standing naked before the court, and everyone would discover that there is a conjurer in their midst."

"That is a drawback," Briana admitted as she worked. "I wish there was a way to fix it, so I didn't have to keep my mind on it all the time."

"There is a way, but not one you ever need to worry about."

"What way?"

"Never you mind. It does you good to concentrate."

Theda borrowed the mirror to approve her appearance. It was rare she had the opportunity. A tall, slender woman in middle age with greying brunette hair and shrewd blue eyes stared back at her.

"You are beautiful, mother. Robert Skinner will certainly approve."

"Don't be ridiculous, Briana. Master Skinner and I are friends. He will not notice or even care." Theda sniffed. "Are you ready?"

"Almost."

A quick wave of her hand at head level created an elegant updo to match the purple gown. Theda sighed. Briana's hair glowed like molten copper, her skin flushed gentle pink with health and excitement. Grey eyes sparkled.

"You are a vision, my daughter. Your father would be proud."

"My father." Briana gathered her cloak towards her. "I wish I had known him. Do you miss him?"

"Every day. You look so like him. Russet hair, grey eyes."

"Was he Blessed as well?"

Theda stood for a moment, still looking at the mirror, but her inner gaze stretched back over the years as images of Ranulph Eglion sifted like melting snowflakes across her memory.

"Yes, he was Blessed. You and he share the same gift. The only people in the whole of Altius Mysterium to bear it. Your father died because of it."

She crossed the narrow space to grab her daughter's arms as, once again, a prick of warning took her memories and turned them into something sharp and watchful.

"You will be on your guard tonight, Briana. Promise me. I know it looks as if nothing has changed since the death of the queen, but believe me, everything has."

Chapter Ten

From the journal of Briana of the Owls, Castle of Air

Darius has been competing all summer long for the King's preferment. He says little about it, but I can see the light of determination in his eyes, and the glares Sir Walter throws his way whenever he gets the opportunity. They hate each other, those two. Like two tom cats, battling for territory. But Darius can beat him. I know it! I wonder what the King will give him for a prize?

An army of servants had outdone themselves in preparing the Great Hall for the Summer's End Feast. Huge stands of flowers stood sentry at regular intervals against the long walls. They had flung back the heavy windows, and a warm breeze perfumed the air, stirring the leaves of the delicate arrangements. A troupe of travelling jugglers swelled the entertainment. Girdred had already seated himself in his usual corner and greeted the court with some of his merriest songs as they entered. Dishes of late summer greens and fluffy white bread lined the tables. Flagons of pale white wine from the northernmost vineyards of Epera, deep red Argentish, and a delicate blue of Oceanian vintage stood in regimented ranks like soldiers. A mouthwatering smell of venison roasted with spices imported from far away Battonia wafted from the kitchens. The sweetness of some sort of unusual honey-based dessert tantalised noses.

"Well, this is pleasant." Robert Skinner elbowed his way into a place amongst the Citizens next to Theda and looked up and down the table with delight, his blue eyes sparking with mischief. "This is not the King's doing, I warrant," he said, reaching as usual for the nearest flagon and offering it around with a profligate hand.

"The King asked my mother for her advice, sir," Ariana said with a giggle, holding out her goblet.

"Ah, yes. Thick as thieves these days, I've heard." Robert nudged her with his sharp elbow, and Ariana blushed, eyes round with pretend shock.

"You mustn't say such things!"

"I don't see why not. It's common knowledge the King must seek another wife." Robert topped off her drink with a practiced flourish and raised his own to his lips. "One never knows. We may be calling you crown princess Ariana soon!"

"Don't tease her, Robert. Theodora is well past the age when she could easily bear the King a child." Theda's voice cut across him, and the delighted smile dropped from Ariana's smooth face.

"Mother! That was unkind." Briana squeezed Ariana's hand in sympathy as the girl's face clouded.

"Only the truth, my dear. Hard though it is to hear." Theda glared at Robert, who had the grace to look somewhat abashed.

"The wine has got hold of your tongue already, Robert," she said.

He grinned. "I wish it would get hold of yours, Mistress. More honey and fewer thorns."

"That's my mother for you, always pricking." Briana stuck her own tongue out, and Theda grimaced. Darius' success had gone to Briana's head. There would be little she could do to curb their excesses tonight, and her company had not even taken their first drink.

The trumpets blared a fanfare as the King entered with Theodora just behind him, along with the rest of his former wife's household and the King's company. Darius and Sir Walter strode a pace behind, Darius loping as graceful as a panther, Sir Walter still angry, judging by his narrowed eyes and clenched jaw. Theda watched her daughter's face as Darius accompanied the King up the long aisle between the tables, and the court rose from their bows. She could not take her eyes off him. Darius allowed the barest nod as he passed their group, his face closed. Did he return her daughter's love? Impossible to say.

Her magical senses whispered danger to her as the lad passed, and she stifled a gasp of horror when she saw the icy coldness that rippled like spilled ink across the rushes in his wake, trailing shadows and darkness. The further he walked, the wider and deeper his black shadow spread until it seemed to bury every courtier, every table, and even the walls in gloom. She shuddered. This was not something she had ever seen before. And the lad, Citizen as he was, with no magical ability, was completely unaware. Rising in the eyes of the world and stalked by evil with every footstep.

She clutched her goblet automatically, swallowing nausea along with the strong wine, her eyes darting to Briana. She would have to say something to the girl, and soon. But besotted as she was, would she listen? And even Robert, gossiping with Ariana, seemed oblivious tonight. She sighed. Was it only ever her? Destined to see the shadows, where others saw only light? How had Darius attracted this darkness to him? Was she even seeing true these days?

Lost in her thoughts and unresponsive to the light-hearted mood of her dinner companions, Theda ate little and drank more than usual. Speculation as to the size and nature of the King's preferment to Darius dominated dinner conversation. Theda had tuned it out long since. All she could think about, all she could see, was that dreadful blackness now pooled at Darius' expensively shod feet. A panting dog waiting for an opportunity to attack. The torches and candles had burned down by about half before the King finished his meal, pushed his platter away, and rose to his feet.

All conversation ceased.

"The time has come for me to make my preferment," Francis looked around at his court, a thin smile twisting his bloodless lips. Theda could see his fist shaking a little where he braced himself against the table.

"In accordance with tradition, I now bestow the following preferments upon the winner of the Grand Tournament. Darius, my Lord of Falconridge, rise!"

Black eyes sparking in the light of a hundred torches, Darius rose with nonchalant grace and strolled to a halt in front of the King. The picture of courtly elegance; he bowed. Briana was not the only young person who stifled a sigh.

"To you, my Lord of Falconridge, in recognition of your surpassing strength, skill, quick wits, and competitive spirit, I give Lordship of the Northern Acres for fifty miles in every direction from your manor at Falconridge, including the rights to hunt, fish, mine, quarry and forest."

A murmur of appreciation arose in the company, along with a series of nods. This was a generous but expected boon, tacking land to his existing estate, which he had inherited following his father's death. A just reward for a mere Citizen. Thinking the King finished, the conversation level rose but died again immediately as the King raised his hands for silence.

"In addition... in recognition of his prowess in saddle and lance, I give the following. Lord Darius will henceforth carry the titles and honours of the King's household. I make him Master of the King's Horse, as his father before him."

Silence. The Courtiers stared at each other in bewilderment. Darius's shoulders twitched in minute surprise. Even he had not expected elevation to high honour in the King's household. He lowered his head in gratitude.

"It is an honour..." he started. The words on his lips died when Francis shook his greying head. "I am not yet finished, lad," he said. Darius stepped back, hands clenched firmly behind his back. The court waited, leaning forward from the back to catch every word that left the King's dry lips.

"In addition, in recognition of the personal service and economic advice you have rendered to me following the death of my beloved queen, I give you the title of Lord High Treasurer."

Pandemonium.

"I protest!" Even as Darius bowed, the feather of his hat sweeping dust from the floor, the now former Lord High Treasurer, Lord Felonius Blount, jumped from his chair, beard waving, fists clenched. His Blessed followers and dependents cried their disbelief. The courtiers turned to each other in complete disarray. Darius, a Citizen, given control of the kingdom's treasury? It was unheard of. Not to be thought of. A nod from the King saw a detachment of guards leave their normal positions against the walls. White-faced, the company stilled at the sound of cold steel leaving leather scabbards. It was only a threat, no swords actually waved, but the courtiers took the hint and regained their seats. The Citizens amongst them shook hands and cheered as if Darius's success strengthened each of them as well. The Blessed could only stare at each other, lost for words, as the King's favourite, disregarded and easily dismissed, vaulted effortlessly over their heads to claim secular power.

At her table further down the hall, Theda's hand shook where she clenched it around her half-empty glass. Briana's eyes lit like stars. Ariana shook her head in astonishment. Robert Skinner raised his own glass in an ironic salute to Darius.

"Well, that is a surprise," he remarked. "A reward for his scholarship. All that knowledge had to count for something. What say you, Mistress?"

Theda lowered her goblet. At the top table, Darius had gone down on one knee, and the King had retrieved the heavy chain of office from Lord Blount. The older man looked smaller somehow, without the weight of gold and silver glaring from his paunch. The company stilled once more when the King leaned across the board, placed the decoration over Darius' shining black curls, and arranged it carefully on his broad shoulders. Darius kissed the King's ring and then stood to face the court, his moment of triumph complete. His cold, conquering gaze clashed with Briana's, and Theda's heart clenched in her chest.

"I say it's a disaster," she said.

Chapter Eleven

From the journal of Briana, of the Owls

My mother has gone entirely mad. She seems to believe that Darius is possessed of some evil force. Just because he's a Citizen and the King seems to like him. I don't care what she thinks. He's clever, and the King understands that. All Darius wants is to please the king and make our kingdom prosper. Sir Walter is furious, and so are the rest of the Blessed. But Darius is fuelled with the need to see the Citizens receive equal status. You'd think the King would have something to say about that, but he's done nothing to stop it. Curious, really, when everyone knows how much he has always discredited the Citizens. I spend a lot of time with Darius, Dupliss and Ariana now. My mother disapproves. I can see the worry in the back of her eyes. I wish she wouldn't worry so. Darius is everything I could want in a husband, even if he often buries himself in his books and disappears for hours and days on end, carrying out his duties.

Francis almost faced a mutiny from the Blessed in the frantic days that followed Darius' elevation to Lord High Treasurer. Whether hunched with her paperwork over her desk or leading groups of children in their studies, Theda overheard many a muttered conversation. Even carefree Robert Skinner lacked his usual buoyant manner when escorting her to dinner and went about his business with a thoughtful frown screwed permanently into his brow. Pointed stares and a general glower followed Darius around the castle, especially when he appointed Citizens to prominent positions within his own office. His friend, Count Dupliss, another gifted economist, gained immediate status as Darius' assistant, and the two talked long into the night in the library, debating strategies and tactics to strengthen Epera's position within Altius Mysterium. Theda could even find something to admire in the young man's achievements as he attempted to equalise the status between Citizen and Blessed, lowering taxes on the Citizens and increasing them for the magical population.

"It won't do, lad," Felonius Blount was heard to say. "After all, there are fewer of the Blessed. What difference are a few gold nobles here or there? Most of the crown's wealth comes from the Citizens. The common folk."

"Aye, and who pays for your grand estates, your temples, and your horses and carriages?" Darius returned with equal relish. 'T'is about time Citizens saw some reward for their hard labour on the kingdom's behalf."

To Theda's despair, Briana remained besotted. As summer faded to autumn, Darius partnered with her for dance after dance, and the pair enhanced many a dull evening in the Great Hall with their quick wits and banter. Small presents from Darius arrived for Briana at irregular intervals. A gold charm for a new bracelet, a posy of autumn blooms, a yard or two of expensive Argentian lace. And yet, as autumn bled into winter, Darius made no further moves. He appeared content to remain an attentive suitor, and Briana herself remained subtly removed from further attachments. The young men of the court could not match the casual display of wealth and high office Darius offered, and their attention drifted to other, more available prospects.

"So, what are his intentions?" Theda asked Briana on the morning of the Yuletide celebrations as they dressed as warmly as possible to brave the traditional Mid-Winter service in the always icy castle temple.

Briana's mouth twisted in a grimace of frustration. "I wish I knew, mother."

Theda sighed. "I warned you on the night of his preferment to stay away from him. Why wouldn't you listen?"

"Yes, I remember how pleasant that conversation was." Briana's bitter tone warned Theda not to tread on the same ground again. "You are just biased against him, for some unknown reason that you refuse to share."

"I told you what I saw, the darkness that followed him."

"And have you seen it since?"

Theda shook her head. "The Mage has shown me nothing more."

Briana raised her chin. "Then perhaps it was a fancy brought on by the wine. Darius wants to make things better for the common folk. You can see that yourself."

Irritated, Theda snatched her cloak from the back of the chair and dragged it over her shoulders. "Of whom, you are not one. Do not lecture me."

"No. That's your job." Glaring at her, Briana fastened her own forest green cloak with nimble fingers and whirled in a swirl of velvet to the door of their small chamber. The scarlet feather in her matching bonnet rippled in the draft from the corridor as she opened it. "I am to be seated with Darius near the King for the service," she said over her shoulder as she left.

The door banged shut, and Theda swayed on her feet, overwhelmed by the animosity between them. One hand reached blindly for the back of her chair for support, and she stared, unseeing, at the merry flames that mocked her from the hearth. Darius. Again. Whether the Mage showed her the strange dark shadow that dogged his footsteps or not, the shape of it lingered to muddy everything he touched. She shuddered as gooseflesh pricked her shoulders under her thick clothes. As in everything else lately, Darius had also won her daughter's heart.

A light dusting of snow twinkled on the shoulders of the congregation as they took their places for the Yuletide service. Seated at the back and shivering in the draft that whispered in under the doors, Theda took comfort in the soaring columns of pale marble. Soft light from tall, narrow windows of stained glass illustrated the legends of the Gods and the making of the four great Magics. Here in Epera, carved birds decorated the walls, along with the sign of the Mage. The painted ceiling depicted more of the same, picked out in silver. The birds circled the Mage, symbols of communication and knowledge. As High Priest Genulph genuflected at the high altar and the service began, Theda's gaze drifted inevitably to the front row, where the King sat in solitary state, his chief courtiers and councillors in the row behind. Her heart ached for him. His crown seemed almost too heavy on his head these days, but she had heard he was now actively considering taking another wife. A possible queen in waiting, Theodora of Wessendean sat directly behind him, Ariana at her side. Further along,

Briana bowed her head, feather bobbing. And beside her, at the end of the row, Darius stared forward, shoulders erect, taking absolutely no notice of the service. She could see his foot tapping from where she sat, impatient to leave.

"Darius has no use for the Gods, has he?" she said to Robert at the end of the ceremony as Genulph blessed the congregation, and the massed crowd lurched to its collective feet, stamping life back into frozen limbs. The King walked slowly down the aisle with Theodora and Ariana behind him. Briana gave her the slightest nod as she passed, her own hand secure on Darius's arm.

Robert's mouth turned down in a wry smile as they waited for the royal party to pass. *"He never did, that I could see. Much more interested in secular knowledge, but that is not unusual for a Citizen. Why?"*

"I'm still interested to know what he found out during his visit to the Restricted section." Theda tucked her icy hand into the crook of Robert's fur-trimmed elbow as they followed the King's party out into a lowering winter afternoon. Snowflakes drifted around them, glistening in the light of the courtyard torches, already lit against the winter night to come. She recognised Jacklyn Sommerton's broad shoulders, pressed to attention against the wall with his colleagues as the King led the way back across the snow-swept flags for the Yuletide celebrations.

"You still believe you saw something following him the night of his preferment." Doubt laced Robert's mental tone, and Theda pressed her lips together in a firm line before she answered.

"I wish I could make you believe me."

"But surely, it's not possible. A Citizen like Darius, attracting the attention of Magic like that?"

"Perhaps he is Blessed, after all."

"It would have shown by now if he was. I don't think what you saw is anything other than a projection of his desire for power. Ambition is not a crime, is it? If it were, we would all be languishing in the King's dungeons by now. The court runs on preferment. People jostling for the King's attention. You know that."

Theda shot Robert a disgusted look from under her brows and attempted to withdraw her hand. He increased the pressure on her fingers at his elbow as he felt her instinctive denial, trapping them momentarily in place.

"*We have no proof that Darius is anything other than an ambitious Lord and Citizen,*" he reminded her. *"And he is now high in the King's favour. To accuse him is to court death. Is that what you want? Think what it would do to Briana and her chances for a prestigious marriage."*

They had reached the Great Hall, laid out for the Yuletide Festivities. The torches in their sconces and candles in the great candelabras hung from the rafters were as yet unlit. Embers of the previous year's Yule log flickered dully in the massive fireplace, waiting for the new Yule log to signify the turn of another year. Holly branches in swags and wreaths adorned the walls. Court musicians waited with Girdred to perform their wassails, blowing on their chilled fingers. Their breath frosted in the cold air. The Lord Chamberlain waited in the gloom only until the last of the Court of Skies took their places before clapping his hands. The heavy doors swung open again on a blast of trumpets, and a solemn procession of eight strong-armed guards appeared, with the massive Yule log braced across their sturdy shoulders. A smile lifted the severe lines of Theda's lips as she recognised Jacklyn at their head. He walked proudly, dark head thrown back, eyes snapping with pleasure at his part in the proceedings. The Lord Chamberlain chose the guards who carried in the Yule log for their strength and loyalty. He rewarded them with the opportunity to stay for the feast and mingle with the Courtiers. Jacklyn already had the look of a man prepared to enjoy himself to the best of his considerable ability.

The guardsmen stopped at the fireplace and manoeuvred the heavy log into place. It thudded into the grate in a shower of sparks and a flurry of flour. Robert Skinner, ever the master of lights, left Theda's side to take a position in the centre of the massive space. He waited, elegant and poised, for his cue from the King. Francis rose to his feet, his chased silver goblet already full to the brim with warmed wine. He held it aloft.

"Masters and Ladies, Wassail to thee. Lift your spirits and your cups! Let Yuletide begin!"

Robert took a breath and extended his arms. Theda felt the swell of his magic as it built in his blood. A room such as this, with a thousand different lights and the Yule Log itself, was a task only a master such as himself could undertake. Theda had not a smidgeon of telekinetic ability, and, despite her carping, she always enjoyed the moment when Robert showed what he was capable of. He glanced across at her with a sparkle in his eyes and clapped his hands. The crowd cheered as the Great Hall flared alive with golden light. The Yule log, smothered with flour, burst into blue flames, and the fragrant smoke that followed drifted across the crowd in a subtle bouquet of pine and apples. Flushed with success, a grin stretching his cheeks, Robert took his seat and reached for her hand. He raised it to his lips and pressed a gentle kiss to the back. Theda blinked in astonishment, and a blush of heat swept her chest under her warm woollen cloak. She stared at him, dumbfounded. He twinkled back.

"A merry yuletide, Mistress. Am I forgiven?"

Theda stamped on the sudden flush of excitement and narrowed her eyes. "Only if you pour me a drink."

Toast followed toast during the feast. Flames from the yuletide log illuminated rosy cheeks flushed with laughter as the wintry afternoon drifted into a freezing night. Midwinter scents of spiced ale, honey, and cloves overlaid the fragrant smoke from the massive fireplace. Girdred performed his most traditional old melodies, and the courtiers raised their voices in song, the rowdy chorus lifting to the hammer-beam ceiling in celebration of the season.

Briana and Darius took to the floor to lead the company in their traditional dances. Francis hunched over a game of chess with his old friend, the Lord Chamberlain, but his foot tapped in time with the lively rhythm of the musicians. No one was surprised when he finally won the game and then looked around the room for a likely partner.

Theda watched from her place in the middle of the reel as he conferred with Theodora. Seated at his side, dressed in rich purple and with a diamond studded headdress perched atop her curls, she leaned in to hear him over the wail of the pipes and fiddles. Whatever he said met with her approval, judging by her enthusiastic nod of encouragement.

The music died at the end of the last measure, and the King rose to his feet. Wine had lent some colour to his pale cheeks, and his blue eyes flashed with a little of their old sparkle as he perused the court. Giggling with Briana in a group with Darius and Dupliss, Ariana did not at first notice his lofty gaze coming to rest on her blonde head.

"Ariana of Wessendean, may I have the honour?" Francis said.

Ariana froze in the sudden burst of conversation as the King made his request. Briana squeezed her fingers and gave her a nudge. Ariana responded with a trembling court curtsey. Briana took a step back and exchanged glances with Darius, who did little more than shrug. The Court of Skies watched like a flock of hungry vultures as Ariana rose and made her way to the dais, where the King stepped down to meet her, a rusty smile on his care-worn face. He nodded to the assembled company.

"Ariana of Wessendean is my chosen partner for the evening celebrations."

As the King took Ariana's shaking fingers and raised them to his bearded lips, Theda risked a glance at Theodora, who sat back in her chair with a secretive smile on her face. For all the world like a well-fed cat. Theda leaned in to Robert.

"That was a game well played. There's your next Queen of Epera," she said.

Chapter Twelve

From the journal of Briana of the Owls

Ariana has promised me a position in her household as second lady. At last, I can leave my mother's cramped old rooms and have some space of my own. It's about time. We only ever seem to argue like cats when we are left alone. If only Darius was still here. The King sent him on some mission or other to the mountains directly after Yuletide. Darius said it was to look at ways to expand our industries there. I wish he'd come back. It's so boring without him.

The wedding of King Francis to Ariana of Wessendean, took place in early spring. Her daughter's face still held a sullen expression as she flung her possessions into a trunk four weeks later..

"I wish you wouldn't worry so, mother," Briana said as she slammed the lid and stood back to make way for a broad-shouldered footman. Raindrops sparkled in his hair as he hoisted it to his shoulder with casual ease.

Theda dusted her hands down the front of her robes and smoothed the coverlet on her narrow bed. Her modest chamber already looked more like a study without Briana's colourful clutter littering every surface, and the grey light outside did little to lift her spirits. Her eyebrows contracted in irritation. "Of course, I worry. I am your mother. I know you are missing Darius. Otherwise, you would be more pleased at your appointment." She crossed to Briana, who stood with her arms folded under her cloak, one foot tapping the floor.

"He's been gone for an age. What can be so important to take an entire season?"

"Have you not received a message?"

Briana shook her head. "He must have found someone else."

"As thick as you two are, I very much doubt it. He's doing his duty for the Crown; that is his job."

"Well, it's boring without him. No one will dance with me in case he hears about it and makes life difficult."

Theda raised her eyebrows. "Surely he is not so possessive?"

"He has his moments."

Theda rolled her eyes to the sky. "And you wonder why I worry."

Briana smoothed her hair and looked around with a sigh, stooping to look under the bed for any stray articles that had eluded her. "You don't need to worry about me. I must go. Ariana is in a state. Something about the visit of the ambassador from Battonia and the proper distribution of his servants to their rooms. Apparently, none of them want to share, and every member of his entourage has brought his horse and his hawk."

Theda shrugged. "I'm sure Theodora can help her."

"I am her friend. She needs me." Briana glanced through the open door to the corridor, scowled at the people passing, and gazed into Theda's eyes. *"She's pregnant, mother."*

"Yes, I know. Theodora is useless at concealing her thoughts. I'm sure any of us with a smidgeon of telepathic ability will have heard by now." Theda picked up her cloak. "Come, daughter, we'll go together," she said out loud.

Arm in arm, the two women strolled through broad corridors crowded with courtiers and servants, taking shelter from the sudden storm that had blown in over the mountains in the last hours. Briana winced as thunder crashed like a cannon against the battlements.

"The Gods know where this weather has come from," she said with a theatrical shiver.

Theda raised an eyebrow. Rain and storm had accompanied the blessing of the priests in the chapel on the morning of the King's wedding, causing the superstitious members of the Blessed to cast offerings at the foot of the Mage and ask his forgiveness for their transgressions. Snow at this time of year was normal. Lightning and thunder, much less so. This storm had rattled around the mountains on and off for nearly a month. She shivered under her heavy winter cloak. Abnormal. That's what the weather was.

"If you are thinking the Gods are angry, you are probably right," she said.

Briana tossed her head. *"Angry Gods or not, I am more concerned about Ariana. She's not well."*

"In what way?"

"Too thin. She's not eating enough. Says everything tastes of ashes and smoke."

"That's very fanciful of her."

"And she's bored with the King. All he ever talks about is how wonderful Gwyneth was."

Theda laughed, although the sound had little joy in it. *"I fear her life is not happy, nor will it be without true love."*

"Very prophetic. Did the Mage tell you that? Why wish something so sad upon her?"

"I do not. Theodora was the one who tilted for a crown. She won. Good fortune and honour attend the name of Wessendean. Surely Ariana is pleased? A Citizen claiming a crown. I have not heard of it in all our history."

A fleeting frown crossed Briana's brow. *"Truly? But you have always said the Gods Bless where they will and that magic does not flow in bloodlines. If it does not matter, why has a King of Epera never married a Citizen before?"*

Theda shrugged. *"Human nature, I suppose. A King may be devout, but it never hurts to hedge your bets, just in case. We would not be logical Eperans if we did not think thus."*

"So then Francis must place a great deal of faith in the Mage if he is content to take the risk."

"Yes, that is possible. Unless..."

Theda stopped dead as a terrible vision pierced her thoughts. She swayed, and Briana cast a worried glance around before she gripped her arm and steered her to a sheltered window embrasure.

Theda stared at the glorious view south to World's Peak without seeing it and swallowed against her dry throat.

"Are you alright, mother? You've gone paler than snow," Briana's voice came from far away. She sounded as if she was speaking from the bottom of a well.

Theda smudged a hand across her face, pressing her forehead where a sudden headache bloomed between her eyes. She grasped Briana's hands. "You go on, my dear. I've just got to check something."

She patted her daughter's hands distractedly and hurried away, back down the corridors to the distant library. The key to the Restricted section bounced against her chest as she panted through the throng.

Theda nodded to Terrence, who was manning the desk in her absence and scurried through the stacks to the magical collection with anxiety prickling her blood like pins and needles. She fumbled with the ancient key as it turned in the lock, felt for a lantern, and struck a flint before slamming the door closed behind her. The books sighed at her entry as she locked the door. She held the lantern higher and looked around. Was it her imagination, or did the collection lean from their shelves to hear her voice, their attention pricked, the atmosphere waiting and watchful?

"I know you have been happy here," Theda said, stifling a sob in her throat with an effort. "But you are in danger. I have to get you out."

Chapter Thirteen

From the Journal of Briana, of the Owls

Ariana is not very well, and she does nothing but moan. Her mother does nothing but wait on her hand and foot and then grumble about her to me afterwards. Life in the Queen's rooms is secluded, and the King hardly ever visits. He's looking ill as well. But Darius is back, and my life can begin again.

Darius spent all afternoon with the King and came away looking like a thundercloud. I tried to ask him what was wrong, but he glared at me as if he hated me. Perhaps his mission was unsuccessful and he has displeased the King.

"You want to remove the contents of the Restricted section? By all the Gods, why?"

Silhouetted against the morning sun filtering through the fresh spring forest that covered the slope below the castle one month later, Robert Skinner stared at Theda as if she had gone truly mad. Theda slanted a hand against her aching head and squinted at him in exasperation. Bird calls rattled against her ears. Easter had come and gone, and the forested slopes were alive with birds feeding their young in spirited relays through the trees. Insects buzzed and whirred. Grasshoppers chorused in rough patches of grass. It should have been a romantic spot, but Theda ignored it all.

"I just explained why. The books are in danger. The Blessed are in danger. If we do nothing now, magic in Epera will cease to exist."

Robert gaped at her. "Don't be absurd, the King would never let that happen."

Theda clamped her hand on his arm and dragged him further down the ride and into a cluster of bushes as a group of mounted hunters clattered past. Hooves pounded the ground, kicking up clods of loamy soil.

"The King is already letting it happen," she said, reverting to telepathy to keep the conversation private. *"He hasn't challenged Darius when he put the Blessed taxes up again. Genulph told me after his theology class yesterday, someone vandalised the Temple of the Mage in Blade two days ago. And the King has done nothing. No soldiers, no personal visit, no decree. It would never happen before."*

Robert waved a long, dismissive hand. "Coincidence. You are clutching at straws to make your theory fit."

Theda bit her lip, turning away. To date, she had let Robert continue to believe her Blessed ability comprised a powerful gift for telepathy. Could she trust him with the whole truth? She jumped when Robert's warm hand closed around her chilled fingers. She could never seem to get warm these days. Three months after the Royal Wedding, sleep eluded her almost completely. Her inner vision thrummed with unwelcome images of the future that took all she had to refute. And still, the Mage presented them to her. Night after night. Temples abandoned and demolished, the bells silent, the priesthood disbanded.

Spectral, skeletal people shuffled away from her into the dark, their faces turned to the earth. Briana lost to her. And Robert. Dear Robert. Dead. How could she bear it?

Her companion took her hands and squeezed gently to claim her attention. "You are tired, Theda, that's all. Please, will you take the sleeping draught the Court Physician gave to you?"

Raising her chin with an effort, she shook off his restraining grip. "I will not. If you won't help me, I will move the books myself. Jacklyn Sommerton's father owns the Tavern of the Falcon in Blade. They are devout, even though they are Citizens. He will help me smuggle the books out if I ask him."

"And risk him being arrested for stealing? He'll lose an arm, if not his life. Theda, you can't do it!"

"Then you help me! You are a member of the Blessed and a professor. No one will question a book or two on your person."

She waited, searching his face for some sign of agreement. Robert stared at her, a muscle in his jaw working, his narrow, clever face pale in the merciless sunlight. Shadows gathered under his eyes. A beetle climbed his collar, its carapace an oily green against the expensive lace at his throat. She raised a hand to brush it away, and half flinched when Robert caught her ink-stained fingers and drew them to his lips.

"You know I would do anything for you, Theda," he said, his voice hushed against the joyous birdsong.

"But will you do this?" her voice dropped to a whisper.

Robert smiled and wrapped her against his warmth. "If you can arrange a haven for the magical collection at the Sign of the Falcon, I will make it my favourite city tavern. Will that suit you?"

Theda stood stiff as a log in his embrace. His warmth invited her to return the hug. Her constant worry for him kept her hands at her sides, and her head bowed.

"What is it?" Robert placed a gentle hand under her chin to bring her eyes to his. "Theda, you are crying. Yes, you are, don't deny it. My dearest, please do not weep. I will help you. I promise."

Theda jerked away, disgusted at herself for giving way to emotion. She straightened her spine with an effort. "I would not ask you were it not so important."

Robert rolled his eyes and brushed her tears away with the pads of his thumbs. "No, my dear. You never would. I'd like to say your stubborn independence is part of your charm."

"As your constant good humour is part of yours. Are you never upset? How is it you continue to deny the changes happening right under your nose?"

Robert shrugged and offered his elbow as he turned back to the ride and the distant castle wall. "Everything changes. It is the nature of things."

She took his arm. "And if it changes more than you would like? What then?"

Her suitor put his greying head back and roared with laughter. A casual flick of his fingers swept across a patch of lily of the valley and sheared them from the ground. Another swirl and the flowers braided together and came to lie in a sweet-smelling, dainty crown around her dark hair.

"Why then, my dear Theda, I will change it back."

Theda sighed as she turned on her heel to start back to the castle and her work in the library. She could do nothing against such boundless optimism.

The steep slope to the outer castle walls took time to traverse. Out of breath at the top, Theda leaned against the barbican wall and dragged air into her lungs. Robert waited beside her, one foot propped on the weathered stone, humming an old ditty under his breath. He nodded in greeting to a stable boy carting straw. Starlings wheeled in the fresh cold air blowing from the north, and below them, the lush leaves of springtime crowned the forests in a froth of emerald and peridot. Beyond, on the northern road that led to the mountains, a small group of horsemen approached at a trot. Eyes watering in the breeze, Theda squinted at the standard one of the party held aloft. Blue and Grey. The colour of the Falcons.

"Darius," she said half under her breath. Even as the words left her lips, a cloud crossed the sun. She shuddered, hugging her cloak around her.

"Well, that's one member of the family who will smile this evening," Robert said, pushing himself off the ancient stone and brushing moss from his cloak. "Shall we tell your daughter the good news?"

Dinner that evening was a merry affair, at least on the past of Briana, who ate at the King's table with Theodora on one side, and Darius on the other. Theda watched, eyes narrowed, as Darius focused his glittering attention completely, for once, on the russet-haired beauty gazing up at him with such devotion. Francis stared ahead, ignoring his young wife as she tried to draw his attention. He appeared lost in thought, as bleak as a man going to an execution. One hand toyed with his eating dagger, turning it end over end. His meal remained uneaten in front of him. His page hovered unheeded at his elbow with a cloth and a goblet of wine.

"A couple of lovebirds," Robert said, following the line of her stare as he sprinkled salt on his meat. "Darius will propose next. Wait and see."

"If he asks my permission, I will say no. Not that there is much chance of that. What is wrong with the King? He looks even more grim than usual." Theda replied, shivering in a stray draft through the partly opened window at her back.

"Do you think so? Is Ariana doing well? Perhaps he's worried about her?"

"Briana has said nothing to me. No. It's the King. I'm sure something is troubling him."

Even as the words left her mouth, Francis scraped his chair from the board. His wife and mother-in-law gaped in astonishment as he left the dais without a word to either of them. His unexpected action had the courtiers rising hastily from their benches, wiping wine and grease from their lips. Robert waved a hand that righted a wobbling jug before it spilled beer into his trencher.

The King stalked out of the Great Hall like a storm wind, and the court gossips snatched the moment to whisper behind their hands. Darius lifted his dark head away from Briana and watched his King's progress out of the room with a smirk dancing behind his eyes. He stretched his neck and rolled back his shoulders. A man satisfied with his world.

Theda's grasp hardened around her own eating knife when Darius bestowed a glorious smile on her daughter and reached into the pocket of his doublet. Briana's cheeks pinked with pretty delight when his hand emerged, holding a silver ring decorated with a large, black stone. The stone claimed attention even across the distance between her place and the King's table. Theda's stomach twisted as Darius offered it to Briana, pushing it carefully onto the fourth finger of her left hand. Her gorge rose in her throat, and she gagged, struggling with the urge to be sick. Robert rubbed her back. His startled gaze flickered between the dramatic scene at the top table, where Briana's head dipped gracefully in agreement, and Theda, who raised her face to his and gasped for breath, clawing at her throat to allow air.

"Theda, by all the Gods." Casting a despairing glance at Briana in the embrace of her betrothed, Robert swung his long legs over the bench. Theda felt herself hoisted into his arms, and her head lolled. With her eyes closed, the scene still played out in her head. Darius bent over Briana, his dancing, dominant shadow claiming her in front of all. And Briana, besotted, charmed. Possessed. Enslaved. No escape for her now.

For the first time in her life, as Robert carried her bodily from the chamber, Theda fainted.

Chapter Fourteen

From the journal of Briana of the Owls, soon to be Lady Falconridge!

I don't believe it! Darius actually asked me to be his wife. Of every maid here, he has chosen me! Oh, happy day! I think my mother must have eaten something that disagreed with her. Master Skinner carried her out of the Great Hall. Darius gave me a curious ring with the blackest of stones. I am not sure if I like it.

Recovering in her bed the next morning, still exhausted and reeling from the dramatic events of the previous evening, Theda was unsurprised when Jacklyn Sommerton poked his head around her door with his normal offering of coal and wood for her grate. More concerning were his shaking hands and the harried expression in his dark eyes.

"Jacklyn, are you well?" Theda asked, levering herself to a sitting position against her pillow and dragging a shawl around her shoulders against the chill in her rooms.

Jacklyn managed a tremulous smile as he lowered the bucket. "More than you, I reckon, Mistress. But you won't have heard the news?"

Theda waved her hand that took in her small bedchamber, with its faded furnishings. "Apart from Briana's betrothal to Darius? I've been here all night, but I can see by the look on your face it is nothing good."

The young soldier heaved a sigh that appeared to climb from the bottom of his army regulation boots. "I hardly know how to say it,"

"Go on."

Jacklyn swallowed, running a hand through the tangled mess of his hair. "They've ordered the temples closed," he muttered.

"What?"

Theda swept back her covers and crossed the room in one quick action that had her head swimming. Face flushed with embarrassment at the sight of her tattered bed gown, Jacklyn backed off into her parlour.

"When. Who has ordered it?" Theda snatched at her outer garments and tugged them on over her head, struggling with her laces.

"Here, lad. Come and help me. Never mind that I'm not a maid."

"Er..."

"Just do it!" She gave him no choice by marching into the sitting room and presenting him with her trim back. Jacklyn fumbled with the trimmings on her gown. If it wasn't for the devastation crushing her chest, the scene might even be amusing in other circumstances.

"Well, go on, spit it out."

"Er... the King...."

"And who else? No, don't tell me. Lord Falconridge."

"Yes. And Count Dupliss."

Stomach churning with unease, Theda sank into the chair by the hearth and put her head in her hands. Jacklyn squatted next to it and poked the dying embers into life. His broad shoulders quivered with tension as he turned to face her. "There's more yet. Do ye want to hear it?"

She managed a grunt. Somewhere at the back of her head, she could hear someone laughing. Jeering. The vision of Darius pushing his ring onto Briana's finger replayed in her mind once more. She jumped when Jacklyn closed her fingers around a goblet, and she took a sip of cold spiced ale that she barely tasted.

"Come on, lad, tell me. Don't be scared." Funny that she should be the one to say that, with her racing heartbeat and the clammy sweat of terror pricking her skin beneath her gown.

"They've formed a brand new guard. The King's Guard, they are calling it. With a new mission. To protect the King."

She frowned. "That's not so bad, surely?"

"To protect the King," Jacklyn continued doggedly, "from the Blessed."

"By the Gods, what has the King got to fear from the Blessed?"

Jacklyn shrugged. "Plenty, when they find out the temples have closed. If the Blessed resist, we are to arrest them. There's talk of sending them to the mines. They want the best soldiers for the King's Guard. Citizens. Only Citizens. They think we don't follow the Mage."

Theda lifted her gaze from the bottom of the goblet, dragging it with difficulty from the hypnotic swirl of ground cloves and the comforting aroma of mace. Her lips thinned as she recalled an earlier conversation with Darius from many months ago. She looked at Jacklyn, face taut with fury. "Darius said something about a plan to get more workers in the mines. I asked him at the time where he would get them from. I can't believe this is his solution."

"I don't want to do it! I've got nothing against the Blessed! Devout, that's what we Sommertons are. It's wrong what they are doing. But I'm just a soldier. What can I say?"

Jacklyn's deep voice rose with distress and Theda leaned forward, placing her hand on his shoulder to still the agitation that twisted around him.

"Hush lad, I know,"

Staring deep into his bewildered brown eyes, she fought to control her own spiralling panic. Unbidden, her fingers wrapped around the old iron key dangling from her neck. Warm from contact with her skin, she drew comfort from the fact that she could still take some action in defence of magic. She drew a breath, then another, concentrating her focus on the Mage, reaching for his presence with her Blessed power. She felt it as ribbons of energy, twisting, shining with white light in the surrounding space. A deep exhale escaped her at the moment of genuine connection. A bridge to the mind of a God. Dust motes swirled in the air and then stilled in the presence of the infinite. Her voice, when she spoke, was older, deeper, and not her own.

"Do you truly follow the Mage, Jacklyn Sommerton?"

His eyes widened with pure terror, but he remained where he was, locked in place by her will. One powerful hand crept to his heart over his heavy serge doublet. He traced the sign of the Mage against his chest with a determined, coal-dusted finger. "On my life, I do," he said.

"Then I have a task for you. You will help preserve Epera's books and its magical knowledge. You will work with the Seer to remove our sacred collection from the Castle of Air, where it is no longer safe. I believe the Sign of the Falcon has long excelled in the art of smuggling?"

The Mage's voice in her throat was inviting, traced with mockery. The all-seeing eye that saw everything and missed nothing. Theda, as trapped by the Mage's presence as Jacklyn, looked on with dry amusement as the young man's mouth gaped. She had to hand it to him. The source of the Falcon's excellent wine and very cheap food had never left Jacklyn's lips. Loyalty to his father and family kept them firmly shut. She gave an internal nod in recognition. He would do very well, this young messenger from the Gods.

"How...how?...Yes." Jacklyn's shoulders slumped in defeat, his voice hoarse. Brave and loyal he may be, but he could not deny the power of the Mage.

"You will do what the Seer says. She will guide you. Only she."

"The Seer?"

"Mistress Eglion. The Seer of Epera," the Mage confirmed, a note of wry amusement in his deep voice as Jacklyn writhed with terror like a beetle on the end of a sharp pin.

"S...Seer..." stuttered Jacklyn between blanched lips. "Yes. If you say so. I agree."

"It is well. Do your duty in my name."

Jacklyn fell to his knees, trembling from foot to foot. Theda shook herself as the Mage retreated, and the dust motes once again danced in the heat from the newly awakened hearth.

She cleared her throat. "Are you well?" she asked in her own voice.

Jacklyn's eyes raised reluctantly from the worn carpet. "Is this you, now?"

"Yes. Me."

"The Seer of Epera? Really?"

"The same. Although you are to tell no one. Are you fit? We have work to do." Alive with the wash of energy the Mage sometimes left her, Theda stood and snatched for her cloak. "We will meet here every morning and discuss how to go about our task," she said, her voice low and urgent. "No one will think to question you bringing me coal.

You've been doing it for months. I will give you books and other items from the collection. You will take them to Blade when you visit your family at the Sign of the Falcon. Someone will take your fancy there. A girl. A boy, whoever. Understand?"

Eyes still glazed with shock, Jacklyn managed a nod.

"Tell your father at the inn; Robert Skinner is about to become a very regular customer. It will take the two of you a long time to transport the collection. I will guard it in the castle, but you and Robert will be in charge of moving it to safety. Not a soul must find out." She reached a hand to him, dropping her voice still further. "This is dangerous work, Jacklyn, and we are at the start of it. The Mage sees you as a willing body, but as a mere human, I must know. Are you willing to undertake this task? You will risk your life for the sake of Epera's magic, and it could come to that as events unfold."

Jacklyn's lips firmed. "Lord Falconridge and Count Dupliss want me to kill the Blessed if necessary. You want me to lay down my life for the sake of them." He stared out of the window at the tilt yards, still dull with shadow at this time of day. Theda waited for his decision. He'd already agreed at the command of the God, but she needed to hear his own choice without coercion or expectation.

When the young man turned to her, it was with the confident stance and squared shoulders of a professional soldier. He put his hand on his sword. "I will join the King's Guard, as they command," he said. "But I will only ever serve the Mage."

Theda let out a breath she didn't know she'd been holding. "Thank you, Jacklyn. I will let Robert Skinner know."

"At your service, Mistress." Jacklyn's nod was formal, but pride shone in his eyes as he crossed the room to the door and entered the busy corridor.

Theda hurried after him, intent on finding Briana. Darius had declared his colours. They could expect no mercy now if their Blessed status came to light. For her own safety, Briana's ill-fated liaison with Darius had to end.

Chapter Fifteen

From the journal of Briana of the Owls

This ring is very unusual. I have never seen a black diamond. Darius told me he found it deep in the mountains. It scares me. It was too big when I first put it on. But today, it has gripped me like a snake. I can barely turn it on my finger, and I feel strange. Not at all like myself. Darius wants me to get the key to the Restricted section. I told him I couldn't, but he said if I truly loved him, I'd find a way. He can be so cold sometimes. Perhaps I should get it for him. He's only a Citizen. He can't use the information from that library. What does it matter if he reads a book or two? Perhaps it would do him good to understand more about the Blessed and our magic. Then he wouldn't hate us so.

Hurrying to her daughter, Theda's magical antennae tingled an alarm at the tense atmosphere in the crowded corridors. Two members of the newly formed King's Guard, outfitted with stiff new uniforms of blue and black, stood to attention at the stout door leading to the King's apartments. Puffed with importance under their plumed helmets, they surveyed the throng of castle dwellers with narrowed eyes, hands tight on the polished wood of sharpened pikes. The Blessed courtiers eyed them with trepidation, leaving a careful distance as they gathered in small, offended groups and waited for the King to hear their protests.

Using the network of servant's corridors, Theda entered the newly built wing constructed for the late Queen. The stonework here still showed the hard lines of craftsmen's tools. The guard at the door to the Queen's suite recognised her and stepped inside to announce her presence. Drumming her fingers on her thighs, Theda tapped her foot and admired the carving on the freshly paneled oak where the Sign of the Mage frolicked with the Sign of the High Priestess, Goddess of Oceanis. A master carpenter had taken delight in his work and then polished it to brightness with bee's wax. She wondered grimly how long it would last before some zealous Citizen tore it down. The guard reappeared and bowed her through, and Theda blinked in the sudden light flooding the room from the ornate, mullioned windows overlooking the busy courtyard. More pale oak panelled the walls, but Ariana had evidently decided against Gwyneth's colour palette of green and gold. A straggle-haired servant standing on a ladder fought to remove the heavy curtains. Her companion, an older woman, rapped out instructions, ready to catch the fall of material. A mound of grey velvet, embroidered with snakes and trimmed with silver brocade, waited to take its place. The standard of the House of Wessendean and now a royal house, for the first time in Eperan history.

A cheerful burst of laughter from the Queen's bedroom and the strum of a badly out-of-tune lute drew her attention from the perspiring servants. She crossed the floor, her feet sinking into the luxurious carpet that covered her footfall.

Ariana had already got her way with the furnishings for her bedchamber. Sunlight glinted off grey and silver drapery at the elegant windows. The Queen's bed frame now entwined Ariana's initials with the King's. A twist of carved adders and the eagle rampant crowned the headboard. Supported by lace-trimmed pillows, Ariana reclined in a state, her growing bump barely bulging the embroidered counterpane. At her side, her face a barely concealed mask of irritation, Theodora held a tray of comfits. Sitting on the window seat, gilded curls striking a warm note amid the pale colour scheme, Briana tried unsuccessfully to tune the lute. All three women jerked around in surprise as they sensed Theda's presence in the doorway.

"Mother!" Briana placed the instrument aside and rose to greet her. The ring on her hand drew Theda's unwilling attention. Obsidian and somehow threatening, its black diamond sat on Briana's frail flesh like a bruise. Briana's youthful face glowed with fervour, grey eyes glittering with excitement. A silk headband embroidered with the crest of the Falcon framed her hair like a crown. She must have conjured it for herself. Theda's skin crawled.

"Did you see last night? Darius has asked me to be his wife!"

"Ahem," Theodora cleared her throat pointedly. Theda tugged her attention away from Briana's feverish gaiety and realised she'd forgotten to acknowledge the Queen. Two pairs of pale eyebrows contracted with irritation, and Theda recalled the adder of their standard. The Wessendeans never did well when slighted. She recovered herself and bobbed a brief curtsey in Ariana's direction. "Your pardon, Your Majesty, I am overcome with my daughter's news," she said between clenched teeth.

"Indeed, and what news it is! We are so happy for her!" Ariana said, taking a comfit and plopping it into her mouth with a satisfied giggle. "Can you ask for wine, mother?"

Thumping the dish into her daughter's lap with a beleaguered air, Theodora crossed the room to order refreshments from the two servants in the outer chamber. "...and get that velvet off the floor, you idiots, it's worth more than the two of you together," she snapped, as she returned to plump Ariana's pillow with unnecessary force. Her blue-eyed gaze bored through Theda's skull.

"'T'is a pleasure to see you, Mistress," Theodora said. Theda expected the next move and was ready with her mental projection of books even as Theodora's thoughts attempted to mesh with hers. She stifled a grim smile of amusement as Theodora frowned her disappointment.

"Yes, now that she is to wed, I came to steal my daughter away on some family business. I hope that is permissible," Theda said.

"We've been talking about her wedding day all morning. They are to marry in the Great Hall." Ariana said, wiping sugar from her cheeks. She gestured impatiently, and her mother hurried to offer a bowl of water and a napkin so she could cleanse her sticky fingers.

"Not the chapel?"

"Well, no. My lord, the King has ordered the temples to be closed. We are henceforth to be known as a secular nation."

"And why is that? Do you know?"

Smooth shoulders creamy against her bedclothes, Ariana shrugged, her button mouth turned down like a petulant child. "As if my lord would share his economic strategy with me! What an idea!"

"Economic strategy?" Theda cut a glance to Briana, who appeared intent on playing with the new jewel on her finger and refused to look up.

"The Lord High Treasurer believes our resources are better utilised to support our industry," Theodora said loftily.

"So you have not heard that dissent amongst the Blessed will lead to their arrest?" Theda said, anger bubbling in her veins like acid.

"Who would wish to speak against the King?" Theodora looked astonished at the very suggestion. Theda blinked, suddenly assailed by the impression she had walked into a roomful of dolls and puppets who had, unaccountably, come to life.

"Who indeed?" she said, "My apologies. I need Briana for just a few minutes."

The Wessendeans nodded a disinterested dismissal, and Ariana turned her attention back to her sweets. "You can have her, but make sure she comes back. We have a wedding to plan," she said.

"Briana?"

Grey eyes raised from their obsessive perusal of the dark jewel, her daughter blinked as if waking from a dream. She dipped an absent curtsey to Ariana and followed Theda back to her quarters, stepping in her footsteps like a shadow, saying nothing. By the time they arrived back in Theda's sparse chambers, the sun had retreated under a blanket of clouds, and a spiteful, unseasonal wind rose to rattle the flags on their poles around the tilt yards and blow smoke back down the chimney. Theda stifled a burst of coughing as it caught the back of her throat.

"Briana, can you still hear me?"

Briana nodded, barely. Theda frowned. Something was definitely wrong here.

"Then speak to me, my dear. I am worried about you."

"No need, mother mine. I am well." Briana replied out loud. She bent to add more coal to the grate. The ding of metal on stone as she replaced the bucket on the hearth clanged like a warning bell against Theda's ears. She smudged her hands over her face, aware of the pressure building in her brow. A reminder she was in the presence of magic.

"I do not think you are. What has happened? What is wrong with you?"

"I am fine. I am to be married to a powerful and wealthy lord of a fine and noble family. Be pleased. Why are you not pleased?"

Theda stared at her only offspring, completely lost. Briana's fingers twisted together, still playing with that blasted piece of rock.

She grabbed Briana's icy hand. *"Leave that alone, Briana. Take it off. I need you to take it off. Now."*

Her heart almost broke, and her blood chilled as Briana batted her away with a shrill cry. "No! You are not to touch it! Leave me alone!"

"I will not. I am your mother. You are in danger, Briana. Please. Take off the ring. You cannot marry Darius."

Briana's icy grey eyes snapped to hers, and Theda stared in disbelief as the joyous light that had always lived in them changed to something else. Something darker. Defiant.

"I will marry him. You can do nothing to stop me." Her voice was a growl. Nothing like her daughter's usual melodious tone. Theda fought to control her horrified expression, reminded once again of the pool of shadow she had once seen lurking at Darius's feet like a pet hound. Or perhaps the most ferocious of wolves.

"Darius doesn't understand Magic," Briana said, her voice musing and dreamlike once again.

"No. He's jealous of those who do, and he believes you are a mere Citizen. You won't ever be able to use your own magic if you become his wife. Is that what you want?"

Briana giggled and continued as if Theda had not spoken. "But he's given me a magic token. So proud of it, he is."

"What is it, exactly?"

Briana shrugged. "It's a black diamond. He said he found the stone buried in the rocks in the Iron Mountain."

Bemused, Theda frowned. Had Darius really given it to Briana with no knowledge of its nature?

Briana caught her thought and looked at her with her eyebrows raised. "He does not know exactly what its power is. The King sent him to find a sample. That's where he's been all this time. But then the King decided he didn't want it, so Darius took it for himself and made it into a ring for me."

"Francis sent him to seek it out?" Mind racing, Theda stared at her in disbelief.

Briana shrugged and twisted the band on her finger once more. "That's what he said."

"I still need you to take it off."

"Very well." Briana turned her hand in front of her mother's face, a smirk disfiguring her beautiful face. The ring vanished.

"There you are. Gone."

"Briana..." Theda's voice held a low warning. She held out her hand. "Give it to me. Now."

Briana scowled and turned away, her slim shoulders hunched like a miser's over a stash of gold. "Why? So you can play with it? No. It's mine. And Darius expects me to wear it. You cannot have it."

Heart thumping with anxiety, Theda tried another tack. "Remember our conversation when you first arrived? Here, in front of the fireplace? You cannot use your gift for selfish reasons, Briana. It will consume you. Conjure a replica if you must, but that stone is evil, and it will turn your gift against you the longer you wear it." She waited. Briana took a couple of paces to the door. The widening space between them yawned like a chasm, and Theda's heart gave a clutch of fear as she imagined life without her bright-eyed daughter.

"Briana, do you trust me?" Her question whispered across the space that separated them. "I serve the Mage, always. My role is to protect this kingdom and all those magically blessed within it. Please believe what I am telling you. That little sliver of stone is evil."

She huffed a sigh of relief when Briana turned back towards her. "You think so?" The dark light left Briana's eyes, and her innocent young daughter emerged from the shadows that had claimed her. The ring appeared again on her hand.

Theda reached towards her once more, hope blossoming in her narrow chest. Had she won? Would Briana listen? She softened her voice with an effort. "Please, my daughter, my heart, let me help you. Give it to me."

Briana swallowed, squared her jaw, and tugged at the jewel. Theda waited, hand held out. Briana wrenched at her finger once more and then stared at her mother, eyes black with terror.

"I can't, mother. It won't come off."

Chapter Sixteen

From the journal of Briana of the Owls

I had a nightmare last night. I dreamed I faced the door of the Restricted section and I had the key, but though I turned it again and again in the lock, the room would not allow me to enter, and behind me, something huge and dark loomed from the shadows and swallowed me whole. Darius has changed since his trip to the mountains. He still nags at me to get him that key. So far, I have made excuses, but his eyes are cold, and when his fists clench and his cheeks turn red, the surrounding air fairly sizzles with rage. His servants are terrified of him. They serve him quickly and leave. My mother keeps the key strung around her neck at all times. Getting hold of it without her knowing is almost impossible. I can't do it. How can I betray her? But what will Darius do if I don't?

The two women stared at each other across the faded expanse of the hearthrug.

"What do I do? How can I take it off?" Briana whispered. Tears welled in her ice grey eyes to tumble down her pale cheeks. "Mother, I'm scared."

Theda's heart turned over. Her daughter, bright, wilful, charismatic, reduced to this fearful child masquerading behind her conjured silks and velvets, playing at being a woman.

Suddenly missing Robert's effortlessly buoyant optimism, she cleared the lump in her throat with an effort. She had to help. But what could she do?

"Let me see that horrible thing on your finger, child," she said. "We need to discover what it is we are dealing with."

Briana's fingers clamped around it. "I don't think you should touch it, mother," she said. "If it's taking hold of me, what could it do to you?"

"I'm not the one wearing it," Theda pointed out, dryly.

"It's still affecting you though, isn't it? I can feel your headache from here."

Theda paused. "You are right," she said. "In that case, let's pay the Restricted section a visit and see what we can find. I'm sure the books will help."

It was on the tip of her tongue to inform Briana of her decision to remove the magical collection from the castle, but knowledge of Briana's struggle with the malicious force that claimed her held her back. The last thing she needed was Briana to go running to Darius.

Stopping in the corridor long enough to send a page to the queen with the news that Briana was delayed, the two women hurried through the long, gloomy corridors to the library. The castle was in an uproar. Frantic members of the Blessed crowded the passageways, milling in panic like ants when the gardener's spade descends. Theda caught the thoughts of the telepathic members of the Court loud above the general hubbub. It appeared the King and his advisers, which included the now hated Darius of Falconridge, and Dupliss, his second in command, had denied the Blessed any concessions. The temples would close. Taxes would remain high. And the threat of force had them all running like rabbits. The Blessed nobility, self-interested to a man, were already debating how quickly they could pack up their trunks, servants, hawks and horses and retire to their country estates, far from the reach of the King's new protectors.

The Great Library should have been full of students at this time of day, but many of the tables in the lamp lit alcoves held empty places. Terrance raised an indignant head as they passed the librarian's desk without stopping. Theda stamped on her guilt at leaving him to fend for himself. A wry acknowledgement twisted her lips as she reflected on her quiet days in the past, when all she had to worry about was a scholar failing to hand back a book on time.

Robert Skinner sat at his normal table, still surrounded by the young children in his care. She threw him a smile, and he was quick to return it, relief at her wellbeing reflected in his warm expression. Something about his calm, unruffled presence steadied her racing heart.

He sent his thoughts after their flying feet. *"Are you well, my Theda?"*

"As you see, my friend. But Briana's betrothal ring appears to have a very negative effect on her. What are your thoughts on the Shadow Mage?"

Robert's alarm at this news buffeted her internal landscape. *"Surely not? By the Gods, what has happened?"*

"Apart from the King ordering the temples to shut and the formation of an additional guard to keep the Blessed in check, you mean? I believe that the stone in Briana's ring holds a link to the Shadow Mage.

Darius hunted it out on the King's orders. We are unsure exactly what that young man knows about it. Jacklyn Sommerton will help move the magical collection, by the way. Do you believe me about Darius, now?"

Fumbling with the key around her neck as they halted, out of breath outside the carved wooden door of the Restricted section, her lips lifted in a small smile as the image of an ironic congratulatory hand clap echoed down their mental connection.

"I have to admit, I know little about the workings of the Dark Mage. Few of us do, these days. Let me know what you discover. I will help in any way I can, of course."

She nodded as she turned the key. The ancient door creaked open, releasing the comforting aroma of warm parchment, spiced with magic. Theda preceded Briana through the entrance, reaching automatically for her lamp. Ever thoughtful, Robert Skinner sent a wave of his energy after her and obligingly lit the lamp before she reached for her flint. The door closed behind them, encasing them in a powerful and watching silence, and Theda held the lamp high as she looked around. At her side, Briana's jaw gaped at the sight of the magical collection. The books disliked Briana's presence. Even as the lamp glow illuminated their faded spines, the books appeared to scuttle further backwards on their shelves. Pages rustled in disapproval, and the silence took on a charged, predatory quality that did not pass Briana by.

"They do not like me, mother," she whispered, creeping closer, and staring at the shelves with haunted eyes.

"They dislike your ring, daughter. Many of these books deal with the power of light over dark and they can sense its presence here. Do not fear. Nothing will harm you."

"Are you sure?" Briana jumped as an ancient artefact shaped like a mechanical beetle in a glass case jerked to life and thumped against its transparent enclosure. Theda gave it a quelling stare. "Almost nothing," she amended. "Here, you take this."

She thrust the lamp into Briana's trembling hands and jerked her head to the back of the room. "Start looking," she ordered. "We need anything that looks as if it might hold information on the Shadow Mage."

Briana nodded and crept forward with the uncertain step of a condemned criminal. The books cringed at her approach. "Shadow Mage?" she questioned, leaning closer and squinting at their titles in the dull light. "What's that?"

Theda sighed. "Did you ever attend to your studies as a child? What were they teaching you at home? All our gods have two faces. One that looks to the light. The other is its opposite, or shadow. Our battle as humans is to accept that the two sides exist and find our own balance between them. Ideally, we would climb, like plants, to the light." Theda ran her hands over the nearest shelves, pulling out titles that shuffled towards her. "But the dark has attractions too and some people find it hard to resist."

Briana lowered the lantern. "Do you mean me?" she asked, sudden ice in her tone.

Arms full of priceless, fragile literature, Theda turned to stare at her with raised eyebrows. "Actually, I was referring to Darius, but take my comments as you find them," she said, acid in her voice.

"Darius isn't evil."

"Perhaps he is not. However, even you must now admit, his actions have led to nothing but chaos."

"He's working on behalf of the Citizens. He's trying to give them a better life."

Theda raised her eyebrows in disbelief and turned back to the shelves. "That is as good an excuse as any, I suppose. The last time I truly encountered him, he was in here, trying to steal a book about magic."

Briana stamped her foot. "Why will you never see his side? It's not fair, mother!"

Theda took a long breath, biting her lips to keep her anger under control. "Darius of Falconridge is a rich, intelligent, good-looking young man with a deep and unhealthy lust for power. That much is true. The Mage has shown me the shadows that dog his every footstep. Whatever his intentions are, I have to recognise my visions of the future from the Mage as possible truths and do what I can to protect us. And you. The boy has just given you a talisman with a direct link to the Shadow Mage, and, intentional or not, he's trapped you and your power with it. Does that mean nothing to you?"

"He loves me!"

Theda closed her eyes as her heart gave a twist of despair. "Does he?"

She winced as the lantern dropped to the floor with a crash of broken glass and a pungent smell of lamp oil. Briana's footfall sounded loud in her ears as her daughter fled the room, smothering a sob against her hand. The rush of her passing stirred the fine hair on Theda's head and left her with the bitter taste of defeat.

Wan light from the library filtered into the room from the doorway as Theda tucked her books into her arm and stooped to retrieve the battered lamp. Straightening her back with a sigh, she leaned against the shelves, struggling against her overwhelming tiredness. Relieved of Briana's presence, the books crept forward once more. At the back of her mind, she was aware of their constant chatter as they exchanged information.

"Well, my friends, what do you think about that? You have met her now, my daughter. Can we trust her?" she asked them.

The library collection shivered. The strange half creature in its glass case huddled to the floor like a frightened puppy. Theda sighed.

"No," she agreed. A world of sadness tinged her words. "We can't."

Chapter Seventeen

From the journal of Briana of the Owls, June 1569

I hate this ring. It's not a jewel, it's a shackle. I've tried everything to take it off. Even when I conjure it away in the privacy of my room, I feel its presence still, like a burglar seeking access to my mind. It's so hard to keep my mental channels shut, I sometimes have to let it in, but then I hardly know who I am. Someone changed and darker. The ring got hold of my mind tonight and I did something terrible. I crept into mother's room while she was sleeping and conjured a replica of the key as it dangled from her neck. I gave it to Darius. He smiled and kissed me. All I could think about was ice and pain. The replica won't last. He will only use it once and after that he will have to give it back. I will tell him I must replace it before my mother finds it gone. He will never know that she has not missed it. But I've betrayed her. Stolen from her and wrecked all her plans and I can never tell her. The Mage will never forgive me, even if Darius does when he finds whatever it is he is looking for. I will never forgive myself. How could I be so stupid? How?

Alone in her room in front of a small fire a week later, Theda leaned her head into her hand, massaging away the daze of fatigue, and turned yet another page. Discarded volumes littered the splintered table top. A pewter plate containing a round of day old bread and a slice of roast boar waited her attention on the hearth. She'd propped a jug of pale beer on the shallow sill outside her window, where the draft from the mountains would keep it cool. As yet, she'd taken none of it, and the sun had long since descended, leaving behind a fretful breeze. She turned her quill absently, scattering random drops of dark black ink on the parchment waiting for notes. So far, it remained resolutely blank.

Frustrated, she sat up and jammed the quill back in her old inkwell. The books had done their best. Over the last few days, she'd concentrated on her questions and let them guide her to the information within their ancient pages. Now, her mind raced with images of the oldest types of magic. Herb lore and the language of rocks and stones. Spells and incantations, wards and balms. Even Professor Winterthorne's book, the one that Darius had nearly stolen so many months ago. offered nothing of interest. All she could find was ways of blocking the power of the Shadow Mage and its ability to invade another's blessed gift. Nothing at all about how to remove the ring from her beloved daughter's finger and destroy the accursed thing for good. Perhaps it wasn't possible.

She pushed her seat back with a sigh, retrieved her sparse supper and had just settled down to eat, when Robert's voice pierced her thoughts.

"Theda, are you well? May I come in?"

She rolled her eyes, levered herself once more from her chair and went to open the door. Outside, Robert lounged against the wall, awkward as a youth, one hand held behind his back, the other clutching a decanter of fine Oceanis wine. He grinned at her, but concern lingered behind his cheerful expression.

"You have not graced us with much of your presence in the last few days, and I've had no chance to ask you how you got on. Briana flew past like a whirlwind in absolute floods that morning." He stopped when he looked behind her at the small mountain of books. Theda bit her lip and stood away from the door to let him in. He smiled again as he handed her the bouquet of summer blooms tied with a silver ribbon he held behind his back. Enveloped in the heady scent of newly budded roses and lily of the valley, Theda closed the door before anyone else could see him.

"Cover for my presence here. I came to see if you had any books you wanted me to take. I see you have." He tugged the commodious satchel that rested across his back and rummaged within its scarred leather folds. "And here. I bribed the King's master chocolatier for these. Your favourite violet chocolates."

Theda narrowed her eyes at him. "Sometimes I wish you couldn't read my mind with quite such ease."

Robert winked and pulled up another chair. *"Shut me out if you can. I challenge you. Have some wine."*

She watched in bemusement as Robert served her food, poured wine, and lounged in his seat with his shoes off and his stockinged feet propped on the hearth. He wriggled his toes.

"Ah, this is the life. Can we stay like this, beautiful Theda? Would you marry me?"

He jumped up and pounded her back as she choked on her wine.

"What? With everything that is happening, you ask me to marry you? What are you thinking?" Theda took another shaky sip and wiped her blurred eyes with the back of her hand.

"Please don't cry again." Robert regained his seat and helped himself to a chocolate. "I just thought this morning how well suited we are, and how well we get on and...."

He stopped when he noticed the horrified expression on her face.

"Are you really that offended?" His face contracted. The absence of his habitual sunny expression caused her a jolt of panic.

"No, no. 'T'is not that," she gabbled, casting about in her mind for an excuse that she might give him that would not cause him too much pain. In the end, a part truth was all she could come up with.

"I cannot be married, Robert. I had not told you before who I really am." She left her chair and crossed into her bedchamber. Robert's eyebrows raised with recognition when she returned, carrying an ornate wooden staff crowned with the carving of a beech tree. Owls and ivy cavorted around its polished length. The surrounding air crackled with energy.

Her admirer's shoulders slumped in defeat and he sighed as he recognised it. "The Seer of Epera's staff. I should have known. What does the Mage bless you with?" His blue eyes shone like sapphires in the firelight. Debating how much to tell him, she allowed herself a small smile as he recovered himself and leaned forward, alight with interest.

She turned the staff in her hand, enjoying the comfort of familiarity with its shape and weight. "Telepathy, as you know. And Farsight. Other abilities that appear to come direct from the Mage himself when required. Have some more wine. I would," she said, taking her own seat and leaning the staff against her knees. She rested her hand against its head and enjoyed the tingle of reassuring warmth that crept into her chilled fingers.

"Farsight? That is rare." Robert dug into the depths of his satchel and produced a long clay pipe and a pouch of tobacco. "Do you mind if I smoke?" he asked. "I find it helps me think."

Theda shrugged. "Of course, if it pleases you."

He smiled his thanks and busied himself with the lighting of his pipe. Clicking his fingers to retrieve a spark from the obliging fireplace, Robert brought the tobacco to life and resumed his former position, head back, feet stretched to the flames. Theda blinked and inhaled the full-bodied warmth of Argent Gold. Robert smoked in silence, his blue eyes half closed, and Theda chewed a mouthful of bread and beef, swallowing it down with the help of Robert's wine. Already exhausted, her head lolled against her chest in the companionable silence.

"Tis a pity," he said, knocking out his pipe.

She blinked awake to find him looking over at her. Firelight danced across his cheeks, softened the lines under his eyes and touched his greying hair with hints of gold. He reached out a long, elegant hand to stroke her cheek.

"I feel I have known you for such a long time, but every day there is more to discover. You are an intriguing woman. So many secrets."

Theda smiled into his eyes even as she cried inside. She had to close all her mental channels to prevent him from seeing the constant, terrifying vision she had of him, and her sense that time was running out for all of them. A runaway cart down the hill to Blade.

"Tell me of your Farsight, Theda. What does the Mage show you in the future?"

Brushing away the gentle caress of his fingers, she moved to the window and gazed across the tiltyards to the distant mountains. Above their familiar jagged silhouette, clouds scudded across a thin, distant moon.

"The Mage shows me many futures, Robert. But he fixes nothing in stone. That is the challenge and the frustration of it. All I can do is try to prevent the worst from happening in the present, to work for a better outcome in the future." A bitter chuckle escaped her as she rested her aching head against the cool panes of glass. "Briana accuses me of trying to control everything. She cannot understand the impossibility of that. I could wish to shape her decisions, or prevent her actions, but in the end, only she can choose her path, just like anyone else."

"So you two had a disagreement that morning?"

She shivered as his arms crept around her and drew her against his chest, dipping his chin on the top of her head. His robes carried a wisp of Argent Gold and the icy crackle of his magic.

Calmed by the warmth of his embrace, still staring out of the window, she related the events of the morning in the Restricted section, her flat tone revealing little of the anxiety that prevented her rest.

"By the Gods." Robert turned her in his arms, his eyes full of concern. "Are you sure she cannot remove the jewel from her hand?"

Theda gestured to the pile of reading material still cluttering the table. "The books have not yet presented me with a solution to that. All I can find are ways to block her gift, so the Shadow Mage cannot access it. Heartsease tea would do it in large enough quantities, but she would never agree to take it. Not Briana. She lives for the power in her veins, tainted by the Shadow Mage or not."

"If the Shadow Mage takes hold of her, she'll resist any attempt to block her magic. I know little of it, but I know it feeds on the magic it finds to strengthen itself, like a parasite, just like the Ring of Justice amplifies the magic of its bearer for good."

Theda nodded, grimly. "She wouldn't let me touch her ring. It's hard to know if that was Briana being protective of me, or the Dark Mage protecting itself."

"And Darius is unaware of the power?"

Theda chewed her lip and turned to her desk, shuffling through the pages of books that rested there. "It's very hard to be sure," she said, taking up her quill and carefully transferring the recipe and dosage for heartsease tea to her ink spattered parchment. "We know he has no magic inside himself, so there is nothing there for the Shadow Mage to feed on. I don't know why Francis sent him to look for it, or even if he believed the search would succeed. Perhaps it was just to get the lad out of the way for a while after the uproar of his preferment. In any event, Francis decided he had no use for it, thank all the Gods. I don't believe he would have shared its magical properties with a mere Citizen, such as Darius."

"Power mad that he is, let's pray the lad never finds out while it is stuck on his betrothed's finger. The Gods know what damage he could do through her."

Swallowing nausea, Theda turned her head away before he commented on her blanched cheeks. Behind her closed eyelids, Robert's corpse still twisted from a makeshift gibbet.

"'T'is late. I should take these books now. I'll take a mount from the stables and ride out to Blade on the morrow." Robert's voice was soft in her ears, tickling her senses, and she pressed her hands hard against her heart that felt nigh to breaking, as if she was attempting to keep it safe inside her chest.

"Theda? Won't you kiss me goodnight?"

She shook her head, struggling to bury a sob. "You should go away from here, Robert," she said, her voice remote and cold as a snowdrift.

"Far, far away, where no-one can find you. Leave the castle. Leave Epera if you must."

His chuckle did little to reassure her. "My dear one, I could no more leave you now than grow wings and fly to the moon. Are you scared for me? Is that it?"

Swiping a hand across eyes that blurred with tears, she raised her face to him. "Everything that is happening now is only the start. The Blessed of Epera will fight for their right to worship as they please. It will not be pretty and many of us will be injured or..."

She couldn't say it.

Robert stared at her, thumbing the tears that trickled unheeded down her ashen face. "Please don't worry about me, Theda. I can look after myself." Raising his hand, he beckoned her eating knife from its position on the table and, with a flick of his fingers, buried it in the back of her cushioned chair. Theda stared at it. The bone handle and chased silver hilt glinted red in the firelight.

"You see, not so helpless after all." Robert's rich baritone soothed her tired mind as he surveyed the knife with his usual confident expression. "If it comes to it, my love, I am more than ready to fight on behalf of the Mage and the Blessed of Epera." He lifted her hand to his mouth and dropped a kiss on its back, his gentle lips soft on her ink marred skin before turning to the table and stowing the books in his satchel.

"You have done with these for now?" he asked, tugging the laces closed.

"Yes, I suppose so, for now."

"Then I will take my leave." At the door, he stopped and turned back to her, his eyes dark with concern. "Your precious books will arrive safe at the destination, Theda, as will I. Please try to rest, promise me that. I'll be back tomorrow afternoon."

She straightened her back. "The Gods go with you, Robert. Please take care."

Expression grave, he bowed, and slipped through the door, leaving Theda to stare at his fragrant, delicate bouquet, already dropping petals like tears to the floor.

Chapter Eighteen

From the journal of Briana of the Owls, August 1569

I'm sure Darius sees something different in me. He keeps asking me if I'm happy to become his bride, with a smirk on his face that knows that I am not, anymore. He's changed so much. Puffed up with importance, so proud of his influence over the King. Ariana is putting more effort into planning my wedding than she did her own, and has her mother running around like a slave on a thousand different errands. I'm not surprised, because Ariana confessed to me the other day that she actively detests the King and is determined to make her mother's life a misery for promoting her to the throne. She thinks it's funny. When I'm in my right mind, I think it's tragic. Anyway, it's impossible to stop her incessant planning. Darius and I are to be wed in just a few weeks. My mother is overwhelmed with tiredness, her face clenched with worry. The shadows under her eyes make her look a hundred years old. And the Blessed are leaving the Castle. They think they will be safe far away in their country estates. Darius just smiled when I mentioned that and told Dupliss to recruit more soldiers to the King's Guard. I wish I had not agreed to marry him, but now I can't take his ring off. What can I do? And I stole for him. If my mother ever finds out, she'll hate me forever. I've ruined everything.

Standing square on Theda's hearth rug two weeks later, with the morning sun picking out shadows under her eyes, Briana tossed the bunch of dried herbs her mother offered her into the fireplace and waved away a plume of acrid smoke. She turned with her arms crossed in front of her chest, chin raised, and a mutinous expression on her face.

"I won't let you drug me! Is that your answer?"

Theda cast her gaze to the low ceiling, where rows of pungent heartsease hung waiting to be crushed into powder and gritted her teeth against her constant fear. "It is the only answer I can see, Briana. I can find no way to relieve you of that jewel, so the only other way is to block your magic, so there is nothing there for it to use. I am trying to keep you safe from what it could make you do, while I continue to search for another solution. "

Briana stared at her, resignation stamped across her delicate features. "It doesn't matter, mother. Not anymore."

Theda frowned. "What do you mean?"

Briana shrugged and wandered to the window. "It doesn't matter. I'll be married soon and out of your way. It will be better for everyone."

"You don't seem happy about it anymore, my dear." Theda poured them each a mugful of chamomile tea from a kettle of boiling water she'd heated in the hearth. Another infusion she thought might calm her daughter's fragile state of mind. Nose wrinkling, Briana took the mug and sniffed it like a suspicious bloodhound.

"What's in this?"

"Not heartsease. I will not give you that drug unless you agree, Briana. Surely you don't think I would? That is chamomile to relax you. Drink it."

Theda took a sip of her own drink as proof, cradling its warmth between her hands. Even in early August, the weather remained cool. Land owners muttered morosely about the prospects for the autumn wheat during dinner. The King rarely left his own apartments, leaving the court to its own devices. In place of the King, the top table was more often crowded with Darius and his cronies. Belly rounding proudly under her robes, Ariana made frequent appearances, enjoying the flirtatious game of courtly love in a way her predecessor had not. Watching her troubled daughter lurch from forced gaiety when she conversed with the queen, to a dazed absence of expression whenever Darius turned his attention to her, Theda's fears had only grown. If only she could persuade Briana to take the tea! Robert and Jacklyn had so far transported around a third of the magical collection out of the castle to the Sign of the Falcon. Even now, another pile of books waited in Theda's trunk for Jacklyn and his daily delivery of coal, but the fate of the magical collection was almost a distraction against the growing torment she saw in her daughter's eyes.

"What is it, Briana? Can't you confide in me, my dear? Is it Darius?"

A shiver ran down her spine when Briana raised her eyes over the rim of her mug. A battle between despair and hope raged behind the crystalline gaze, but Briana had cast a fortress around her innermost thoughts. Not a trickle escaped Theda could latch on to.

"Please, my dear one, I only want to help."

One copper eyebrow raised to acknowledge Briana had heard her. Apart from that, nothing. Taking another sip before leaving her cup to steam on the windowsill, Briana dipped a graceful, formal curtsey as she prepared to take her leave.

Theda grabbed her daughter's crimson brocade sleeve to detain her, the material rough against her fingers. "Don't leave, Briana. We can talk about whatever is troubling you."

Briana eyed the crush of her dress with distaste and shook herself free. "Talking won't help, mother. Not anymore. We both have to face it. This thing has dug its claws into me. There is nothing we can do to take it off, and I won't block my magic. It is the only thing I have that makes me myself. Please try to understand."

"What have you done, Briana?" Theda asked, suddenly more rattled than she wanted to admit. "This is not you speaking. The daughter I know would not give up so easily."

Throat working, Briana swallowed. Her black diamond seemed to suck the sunlight out of the narrow room as she brought her hands to her face. "I have done nothing," she said, her voice muffled. "Nothing except fall in love."

"You do not have to marry him, Briana." Theda's voice was equally hushed, her magical senses pricked with alarm, "give yourself some time, we will find a way through this, together. I promise."

Briana dropped her hands, and Theda stepped back from her, horrified at the sadness pooled deep within her eyes.

"You were right, about me, mother. You warned me my pride would be my downfall." Briana's mouth contracted in bitter lines that added years to her age. "I thought I could bend the world to my whim, and now something far more powerful has wormed its way inside my mind."

Theda's eyes widened. She wrapped her arms around her daughter, hugging her frailness hard against her heart. The edges of the iron key she still wore day and night pressed against her chest bone. "You must fight it. Fight with everything you have to prevent it taking you over."

Muffled against her chest, Briana's breath warmed her skin. "I do, mother. But it is clever and I am weak. That's how it works. It burrows inside your mind and searches you for failings. It loves your doubts and your fears, and when it finds them, it rejoices because that's what makes it strong."

Heavy with sorrow, Theda rocked her daughter in her arms. "I am so afraid of what will become of you should you marry Darius. It's clear now, he has no love for the Blessed, and if he finds out who he has married, no good will come of it for you, or any of us. Please, Briana. Call the wedding off. Don't give him power over you."

The space between them grew cold as Briana withdrew from her embrace and looked at the tangle of herbs hanging from the ceiling as they twisted lazily in the fire's warmth.

"This Heartsease. What exactly will that do to me, if I choose to take it?" she reached out to rub the still damp leaves together, wrinkling her nose at the bitter scent.

"In small doses, it would calm you. A medium dose helps you forget the memories that cause you pain." Theda paused as Briana's dull gaze brightened slightly at this news.

"And a large dose?"

Theda heaved a sigh that shuddered from the roots of her soul. "Taken continually, will smother your magic and make you forget you ever had it."

Silence, like ice over a winter lake, stretched between them. Theda held Briana's gaze. There was nothing else she could offer that could take away the pain she saw in front of her. Conscious of her pounding heart, she waited for her daughter to speak, willing her the strength to make a good decision.

"I will break the engagement with Darius."

Theda inclined her chin with a jerk of relief as she released a held breath. "And will you take the heartsease tea?"

Another long pause and her hopes climbed tentatively from the ashes of despair as Briana once again reached a trembling hand to the nearest bunch of greenery. Theda sent a desperate prayer to the Mage for courage and had to prop herself against the back of her chair when Briana withdrew her hand and looked her straight in the eye. The smirk of the Shadow Mage played like a possessed child in the ink of her pupils.

"No," she said.

Chapter Nineteen

From the journal of Briana of the Owls, August 1569

Darius must have found what he wanted in the library, because now he knows this stone has some power over those Blessed by the Mage. Sometimes I feel he watches me like an ant under a magnifying glass, turning on the heat to see what I will do. I've come to see there is more than one Darius. To all the world, he's the charming courtier, witty and erudite and sporting, but another person lives under the surface. I call him The Watcher. He's the one who likes to set the puppets dancing, like bodies on a gibbet, just to see them spin. It makes my blood run cold. I have to break this engagement. I have to. Mother is right. There is evil somewhere inside him. He suspects I am one of the Blessed. And he observes me out of the corner of his eyes, waiting to see me break. None of the Blessed are safe. Not me, nor mother. No-one. Not any more.

Head down at her work in the library, wrapped in a shawl against the unseasonal squall hurling rain at the ornate windows and uncomfortably aware of the chill draft across her booted feet, Theda was unprepared for the arrival of the King's Guard.

A ring of hardened leather boots tramping across the stone flags jerked her head from her books and she slid backwards in her chair to meet their captain's terrifying, ice blue glare. The man headed a group of six hard faced soldiers, clad in bright armour and stiff new cloth decorated with the king's standard. Eyes filled with stony purpose, they stamped to a halt in front of her desk and stared down. Fear clutched her gut and her eyes darted to the space where Robert habitually sat, encouraging his pupils through their lessons with his stories and patient demonstrations of skill. Thanking all the Gods that he was not in the library at present to witness this incursion, she laid down her quill, willing her fingers not to tremble.

"Good day, gentlemen, to what do we owe the honour?" she enquired pleasantly, although her magical senses pricked at the intrusion. Already, she was projecting a mental warning to any of the Blessed nearby who had the use of telepathy. The message was simple to any who could hear it. *"Stop all magical activity now!"* All she could hope was that young Terrence Skinner, gifted with telekinesis but not telepathy, was close enough to another member of the Blessed who would hear her warning. But chances were he was deep in some obscure section, levitating books to the tall shelves with just the power of his mind.

"Greetings, Mistress. The King charges us to search the library for members of the Skinner family."

Theda arched an eyebrow, and her stomach took a terrifying dip into the realms of terror. She raised her voice, in case Terrence was in earshot. "The King wishes you to search for the Skinners? Are you sure?"

"Those are our orders, Mistress, direct from the Lord High Chancellor. Do you have a problem with us carrying out our sworn duty in the King's name?" His gloved fist slid to the pommel of his sword, just visible under the heavy serge cloak embroidered with the King's eagle. Theda swallowed against her gorge and narrowed her eyes. The King, sending soldiers against his own people. Against Robert and Terrence? This was not happening in his name. She would wager her soul on it.

"Why are you looking for them?" she asked, eyeing the fist on his sword with acute trepidation.

"It's not for you to worry about, Mistress. Orders are orders."

"There are no members of the Blessed here," she hedged. "They have all left the castle in recent weeks."

The man raised a disbelieving eyebrow and waved his hand at his comrades. "Search the library."

The group dispersed, and Theda watched them slink like a pack of starving wolves into the stacks. Unaccustomed hatred bubbled in her chest. Their leader remained, hand still on his sword, and regarded her stonily from under his ridiculous bird plumed helmet. Theda stifled an urge to snatch up her staff and beat him over the head with it until what passed for his brain leaked out of his ears. Luckily for her and for him, it remained securely locked in her room, hidden behind her bedhead.

"What are you about, man?" she hissed at him. "The Skinners are no threat to the King. Take me to him. I will vouch for every member of my staff and students, Blessed or Citizen."

"Keep going like that, mistress, and the only thing you'll be vouching for is a swift trip to the Northern Mountain mines. Do you feel like taking that journey now? In an open cart? With winter starting up in those hills and just the clothes you stand up in. Because I can arrange that, if you like." Sure of his orders, he appeared almost amused by her protest. Theda clenched her jaw so hard her teeth hurt.

"I am the Chief Librarian in the Great Library of Epera. Terrence Skinner is the king's loyal servant. Surely my word must count for something." Even as she argued with the man, her ears strained to hear evidence of what passed in her domain. From close to, a panicked whisper hissed around the students, still in attendance. Part of her was glad so many of the Blessed had already seen the way the wind was blowing and fled the castle. Where Robert was at this precise moment, she did not know. He'd left yester eve with one of the last remaining batches of books and had yet to return, thank all the gods. The image of the almost empty Restricted section, protected only by the key dangling around between her breasts, loomed so vividly in her imagination it surprised her the guard did not see it. But Terrence, as stubborn and over confident as his father, remained. And he'd protect the magic of Epera with his dying breath. That much she knew.

Still holding her eyes and daring her to try anything, the captain of the King's Guard stood tall and easy between her desk and the door. Even as she estimated her chances of dodging around him, her blood froze in her veins as a shout of triumph went up somewhere in the mathematics section. A howl of rage and the ominous rumble of an avalanche of books accompanied it as they made an unscheduled descent from their shelves. Theda ducked automatically as a blizzard of torn pages and heavy, metal trimmed book covers whistled like cannon balls from the depths of the room.

"Catch him!" The Captain bawled his orders with zealous determination burning in his eyes, and tore off down the aisle, batting aside the flying missiles and unsheathing his sword as he went. Theda waved wildly at the door to encourage the remaining students to leave and barrelled after him, determined to do something, anything, to prevent them from taking Terrence.

The boy was powerful. It was rare to see a telekinetic gift used so effortlessly and with such control. Theda darted sideways to avoid more cartwheeling books as they shot down the aisle towards her, but even as she closed in, she shook her head. Too much magic, too quickly. He'd burn himself out within minutes. No-one could keep this up without the amplification provided by magical artefacts such as the King's Ring of Justice, or the Queen's Ring of Mercy, which, she realised, she'd never seen on the current Queen's hand. She had no time to ponder this as she slipped between two empty shelves and caught up with Terrence and the group of men who surrounded him. The young man's eyes burned with the rage of a cornered tiger. Slender frame pressed against the door to the restricted section, his chest heaved with exertion, long hair tangled and damp with sweat. He'd given the soldiers a good run for their money. One man slumped in a heap, buried in the contents of the mathematics section and a splintered portion of its heavy oak shelving. Blood pooled around his head, staining the flags. His sword lay nearby, dropped from his flaccid fingers. Another soldier sported two black eyes and a murderous expression, whilst another man's face dripped with blood from a broken nose and at least a couple of missing teeth.

Terrence's head jerked around as she appeared at the edge of the group, and his eyes widened in dismay. Heart pumping, Theda ignored him. Gathering her own energy, she dropped into the mind of the Mage and a surge of energy rose to lift her cloak and raise the hairs on her arms. Eyes wide with revelation as her power shimmered, Terrence yelled at the soldiers, rage in every syllable.

"What do you want with me? I've done nothing!" His voice, less deep than his fathers, but just as confident, rang around the ruined bookcases to snare their attention, and Theda raised her hands, ready to defend her territory. Her magic, and her right to wield it.

"That's not true, though lad, is it?" The nameless captain of the guard moved forward with contemptuous grace, his blue eyes hard on his quarry, his tone both conversational and insulting, all at once. "You may have done nothing before, but you surely have now. There's a difference, you see. Look at my man there," he waved a lazy hand at the unconscious soldier. "And these, here, with the black eyes and broken bones. So you see lad, you'll have to come with us, because you are guilty of using your Blessed gift to injure another person. And that's an arresting offence and always has been."

Terrence's eyes darkened with fear, but somehow he raised his chin enough to glare at Theda where she still stood, ready to wreak her own brand of havoc. The lad shook his head in her direction, causing the soldiers' heads to turn on their shoulders in surprise.

"Nay, Mistress," he said. "You can do naught to save me. Let them do with me as they will."

She lowered her hands to her hips with an effort. "Terrence, this is not right. You have done nothing save defend yourself from an unjust arrest."

The look he gave her was bleak in the extreme. "You've seen the way the land lies now, Mistress. I am Blessed, and it's clear that the King has turned against our kind for whatever ill reason of his own. There is nothing you can do." His dark eyes bored into hers, their message clear. Theda had never shared her status with him, but the lad had guessed, and he was doing his best to save her to the limit of his ability. Her gaze drifted from him to the symbols of the mage that adorned the door to the Restricted section, where the rest of the precious magical collection still waited for transportation to safety. She drew a breath into her lungs, willing her power back to sleep, even as her eyes welled with tears. All she could do, as the lad marched tiredly away to his fate, surrounded by an armed guard, was wonder how she could tell his father.

CHAPTER TWENTY

From the journal of Briana of the Owls, September 1569

I tried to break my engagement today. I took supper with Darius as usual, and then we went for a walk around the castle gardens. It should have been romantic, I suppose. He was asking questions about the wedding, and what Ariana had planned for it. just as if he hadn't sent soldiers into the library for Terrence Skinner. I couldn't stand it anymore. So I took a deep breath and just told him, straight out, that I wished to dissolve our alliance. And he looked at me, right into my soul, and said unless I marry him, as I promised, he will go straight to my mother and tell her I gave him a key to the Restricted section. I can't let him tell her. I can't bear her to know how deeply I've betrayed her. He has me. I am lost.

Working alone by the light of a single lamp, Theda had barely made a dent in the mess created by Terrence's arrest by the time the supper bell tolled. A further detail of soldiers and a physician had arrived to collect the injured man from the wreckage. Now, all around her, the abandoned library stretched into inky darkness. Back aching, she toiled to stack pages together in orderly piles, using all the power of her intellect to determine which page belonged to which book. There was nothing she could do about the felled shelves. Perhaps Jacklyn and a few of his men would help her stand them upright. Would the King commission new ones for those damaged irretrievably? How could she ask? Ignoring her protesting stomach, Theda laboured long into the night. Restless with worry and anxiety, her bowel churned with guilt as the piles of paper grew. Each loose page a reminder of her failure to protect Robert's son.

Tugging herself upward from a stiff crouch somewhere around midnight, she cocked her head at the sound of the door opening. Her belly coiled with dread. Conscious of overwhelming fatigue, she leaned on a shelf for support.

"Theda, are you in here?"

"Robert. Thank the gods". She blinked in the sudden light as the lamps blazed alive and her shoulders knotted with tension at her first sight of him. Robert strode down the rows towards her, his face white with rage, hands clamped into fists by his sides.

"What happened? Where is my boy?" His mental voice roared in her head, and Theda stifled a wince as she strengthened her internal defences against him.

Robert glared at her as he closed the distance between them. Theda's eyes narrowed. She moved away from the shelf and faced him with her hands on her hips. Achingly aware of the pain behind his anger and the turmoil in his heart.

"Don't you dare shut me out. You should have helped him. Why didn't you help him? Too afraid of what people might find out about you?"

She stood her ground as his hands shot out to grab her shoulders. Up close, anger glazed his sapphire eyes. The surrounding air sparked with barely contained magic, and she had an instant to regret the result of her labour as Robert jerked one hand at the carefully stacked loose pages and scattered them once more, like autumn leaves, to the edges of the room.

"You and your precious books. What are they worth, Theda? Are they worth Terrence's life? What about mine? What about Briana's?"

Buffeted by the force of his anger, she twisted in his grip. "Let go of me." The iron in her own voice surprised her as she took a couple of steps back and impaled him with her own glare. "I am the Seer of Epera. My role is to protect this kingdom and its magic from the forces that threaten it. It is not to prevent others from making their own decisions and suffering the consequences of their actions, no matter how much I might want to. I told you this before."

Robert scowled at her. "How can you stand there as soldiers arrest my son and do nothing?"

Her eyebrows contracted in a frown as fierce as his. "Oh, do not mistake me, Robert. I was quite prepared to sully my contract with the Mage and go to his defence. I started to, in fact. Your son did not wish it. He accepts he has injured other people using his magic. Citizens, no less, who could not retaliate equally. It is one of our first laws, Robert. You are a tutor. Do not stand there and tell me you don't know it in the roots of your soul. It is the first thing we learn as members of the Blessed with active gifts. Terrence understands that. He went with them."

"But for what reason did they seek him in the first place?"

She gave him a curt nod. "Exactly. That is the real question, is it not? The soldiers say they are acting on the orders of the King. Personally,

I do not believe it. There is only one person behind it, and we both know who it is."

Mouth twisting at the logic of her statement, he nodded. Her shoulders relaxed by degrees as his brow cleared of the overwhelming rage to be replaced by confusion. "The thing is, to date, there has been an uneasy truce between the Blessed and the Citizens. Historically, our role is to use our magic to defend our nation and all its people. And now you say that we may not use it even in our own defence."

Theda frowned. "Every balance only exists on a sliding scale. Over time, I fear the Blessed have forgotten their own contract and believe themselves better than those they are morally obliged to defend. Hence all the uproar among the Blessed about the King's choice of bride and Darius's preferment. Perhaps Darius wants to give us a taste of what it feels like to be a Citizen. I could understand that."

Robert's eyebrows raised as he surveyed her. "I cannot," he said flatly. "I commend your logic, but I strongly disagree. The King's Guard can't go around arresting members of the Blessed just because they are using magic. Closing the temples and denying followers of the Mage access to their worship cannot be right. I watched an old woman arrested in front of my eyes in Blade yesterday afternoon. All she had done was place a posy at the foot of the statue of the Mage in the Town Square. If that's what Citizens do when given the power of the law, I can't help but feel we were better off before."

"That, I agree with. I am going to ask for an audience with the King. Only he has the authority to stop the balance of power shifting too far in the other direction."

"It is late. He will be asleep."

"I know. I will go in the morning."

"We will both go. Terrence is my son."

"Of course." Tucking a stray strand of hair behind her ears, Theda surveyed the snowdrift of newly scattered parchment. "In that case, having destroyed all my hard work, you can use your blessed gifts and help me clear up this mess."

Chapter Twenty-One

From the journal of Briana of the Owls, September 1569

By the Gods, I do not know what is happening to the kingdom anymore. Darius stood right next to me at the window this morning as they transported the first prisoners, including Terrence, to the mines. I had to move away from him. He's hard to read at the best of times, but today, his expression was almost joyful. Gloating. As if he'd just won the King's blasted preferment all over again. I don't understand him. To deal with him is to marvel at the exterior he presents, like the most exquisite porcelain dish, only to find a seething mass of scorpions and ice when you lift the lid. And this is the man riding roughshod over our King and our people. Over me. Poor Terrence. What will become of us all? Why did I not listen to my mother? Why?

Dressed in her best court finery for an audience with King Francis the next morning, Theda chewed her lips as Robert paced the length of the highly decorated corridor that led to the Throne Room. Sleep had clearly eluded him. Creases marred his usually neat robes, his hair stood on end. Shadows blacker than sorrow lined his sapphire eyes.

Word had, of course, already circulated of the Skinner's fall from grace. Theda's eyes narrowed with displeasure at the smirking faces of the newly elevated Citizens, who clustered in groups to discuss the latest news. They avoided Robert's tall, stork-like figure as he turned and retraced his steps, his hands clenched at his sides. Theda lowered her mental defences enough for him to contact her should he wish to, but this morning, Robert's magic clenched as tight as a fist, misted with anger. Her own hands twisted uselessly in her lap, her mind's eye replaying the harrowing scene as Terrence took his place in the ramshackle cart bound for the Iron Mountains just that morning. The accompanying guard did not need to bind him. No shackle could have contained his ability, anyway, should he choose to use it. But the lad remained loyal to his oath, taken at sixteen, just two short years ago. He'd broken it once, and this was his punishment. Harsh though it was. Her lips thinned further. A fine would have been enough. Not this... ridicule and pain and banishment. Potential death. Raising her gaze to Robert's, Theda shuddered at the rage she saw there. It had never occurred to her that laughing, optimistic Robert Skinner could be violent, but as time passed and the guards in front of the King's door did nothing other than stare into space, his tension only grew. The air crackled with magic as he reached her, stopped as if to say something, and then whirled again down the corridor, his cloak billowing around him like a storm cloud.

Courtier after courtier answered the summons of the Lord Chamberlain to attend their King as the morning dragged out. When the summons came for the noonday meal, Theda levered herself off her hard wooden seat and rubbed her abused haunches. The King's audiences for the day were over. He would not grant their request at this moment. Robert's bleak gaze matched her own as she finally joined him in the middle of the corridor.

"We will try again after the meal," she said, rubbing his sleeve in a curious gesture, half placating, half hesitant. Robert pierced her with a glare and retraced his steps to stand in front of the guard.

"I am not leaving this spot, Theda," he said. "I will see the King, no matter how long it takes. He can recall them. Send a fast horseman with a message, send a bird."

"Robert," Theda began and stopped. She watched, helpless, as Robert dragged his hands through the tangled mass of his hair.

"How can he banish and imprison my son? Loyal member of the Blessed, as he is. I don't understand it." Robert loomed closer to the men guarding the King's chambers who stood to attention, one on each side of the heavily carved doors, pikes raised. Even as she watched, the pikes crossed in front of the door, the guards' message obvious. No entry.

"Robert," she repeated more emphatically. Her voice felt rusty with disuse, choked with her fear for him. "You must come away, my dear. You can do no good like this. Let me talk to him on your behalf."

His jaw tensed under his scrubby beard. "I must, Theda. If it were Briana, you would do no less."

She raised her eyebrows and then sighed and returned to her hard seat.

"You don't have to wait with me. Eat."

"You know I won't do that, Robert."

Silence crept between them as the corridor emptied of people until all that remained were the stoic, blank-faced guards. Theda jumped when the doors finally creaked open, and her heart sank when her head jerked up to stare into Darius's mocking face.

"Master Skinner, Mistress Eglion." Darius sketched a bow, icily polite, as usual. His dark eyes slid over hers as slick and sticky as blood, and Theda's skin crawled. "His Majesty will see you now."

He nodded them through. Robert strode past him with his eyes fixed ahead, not even bothering to meet his gaze. Theda caught the full bore of malicious triumph in Darius' eyes as they tracked Robert's entry into the King's domain. A cat with the juiciest of mice in its maw. Swallowing her fear down, gathering her connection to the Mage to her like armour, Theda followed Robert in.

Francis slumped on his throne at the end of the long room. Gone were the days when he sat tall and erect against his royal blue cushions, and the chamber echoed to the boom of his laughter. Theda's boots tapped rhythmically on the tiles marked with the sign of the Mage. Dull sunlight bled traces of red and blue from the famous stained-glass windows, four to a side, that lined walls decked with ancient shields and curious, curved swords. Almost empty of people and hemmed on both sides with members of the King's Guard, every small noise echoed from the hard surfaces. Robert strode onwards before her, dusting the tiles with his cloak, his hands still clenched at his sides. Magical senses laden with dread, Theda hurried in his wake, regretting her decision to leave her staff behind. Darius's dark shadow trailed her hurrying footsteps, clouds chasing the sun. Even now, she could hardly believe the lad had no inkling of it.

The small group gathered at the bottom of the shallow flight of steps that led to the dais. Francis roused himself from a near doze to peer at them, rubbing a shaking hand across his pale, stubbled cheek. As Robert bowed, Theda curtsied, hiding the shock she felt at the sight of her King. She'd not thought it possible the man could lose more weight. Even as his wife waxed large in her pregnancy, her husband shrunk. She rose to her feet and risked a glance at Robert, who darted a look to her that bespoke his own alarm.

"Master Skinner, you wished to see me?"

"I do, your Majesty. I would like to ask a boon regarding my son, Terrence Skinner." Robert's tone was respectful, hushed even. Theda nodded with approval. No one could take offence at this, surely.

"Terrence Skinner? Is that the young man who caused such mayhem in the library? That is his name?"

All Theda's magical instincts snapped to attention at the King's vague manner. As Darius stepped closer to whisper in his King's ear, every hair on Theda's arms crawled upright. Unbidden, her trembling hand reached for Robert's sleeve as she used her gift to reach the King's mind. Frowning, she abandoned caution and tried harder to push past his defences. Even someone as skilled as Francis would have given way under the onslaught. Robert opened his mouth to make his reply, and Theda schooled her expression to blandness with an effort that made her dizzy. She'd tried her hardest to reach the King. But his mind was as closed to her as any normal Citizen. His telepathic ability was not just submerged; it had vanished. There was nothing there.

"Well, what is it?" Francis shrugged away from Darius and levered himself upright, glaring at Robert. "What do you wish of me?"

"Someone has unjustly accused my son of disloyalty to the Crown, sire. I am here to vouch for his complete loyalty to you and to Epera," Robert replied. He stood stiff and still. The tremor in his voice told Theda he still struggled to contain his temper.

"Indeed, are you? But what of the lad's actions, hey? I hear he decimated the library. Destroyed it with his power. And those sent to seek him narrowly avoided death. Tell me, Master Skinner, is that the loyalty you speak of? This unbridled act of aggression against my soldiers sent to search for the lad. What of the oath he took to do no harm to others with his magic? Hmm?"

Robert's eyes widened, suddenly speechless. His mouth worked, but no sound issued forth as he struggled to marshal his arguments. Theda took a deep breath and stepped forward.

"Sire, if I may, the lad merely acted in his own defence, as any might do if unjustly accused. In all my years of knowing the Skinners, none of them has ever displayed the slightest disloyalty to you or the throne. What could have caused you to doubt him?" She was careful to keep her gaze from drifting to Darius. The young man stood at ease by the throne, confident in his position as adviser to the King, but she was sure he was smirking at her.

Francis cast a rheumy glance in her direction. "I would think you would be more disturbed, Mistress Eglion. Your library, as I understand it, is in a state of disrepair."

"Nothing that I cannot mend, your Majesty." She spoke through gritted teeth, and the King surveyed her with disbelief, one grey eyebrow raised.

"And are you loyal to the Crown? How can I be sure, these days, who is truly loyal when my subjects question my laws and refuse to obey them?"

Theda ignored his question. "In what way did Terrence Skinner show his disloyalty to you that would cause you to have him arrested?"

"The guards went to look for him, Mistress, not to arrest him." The King's tone was flat, almost disinterested. "He earned his arrest himself when he used his power against them. It is clear. The punishment is just. He will go to the mines as a slave and work there until it is my pleasure to release him."

Robert lost all colour as he braced against Theda, his wide mouth screwed to a thin slit of rage. Too late, Theda caught the blast of his power as it erupted from him. She gasped in horror, arms reaching out to stop him, but there was nothing she could do. Robert screamed at the top of his lungs, and the decorative armour crashed from the walls. The priceless stained-glass windows shook in their frames as the ancient swords, once brandished by legendary Eperan soldiers, screeched from the iron brackets that held them to roar across the room. They hung in the air to point at the King, iron tips trembling.

"Robert, don't!" Theda yelled across the startled shouts of the armed guard as they raced from their stations towards the throne.

Francis eyed the pointed swords with something that looked almost like admiration before his gaze dulled once more.

Darius straightened to his full, commanding height, wearing a complex expression that combined jealousy, fear, and a terrible, malevolent satisfaction.

"Threatening His Majesty the King," he drawled, jerking his chin at the stunned guard. "Take him out and hang him."

Chapter Twenty-two

From the journal of Briana of the Owls.

The king forbids us to leave the Queen's suite this morning. There is no explanation, but I can guess what has happened. We are pretending everything is normal. I am writing this. Theodora is reading. Ariana has placed a pack of cards in front of me, demanding attention, as usual. She wants me to play. I can hardly see them. Queens bleed into knaves. Whatever happens, it's will be my fault. All of it. Oh mother, what have I done?

"No! Your Majesty, please!"

Theda barely recognised the screech of pain in her voice. Robert's face transformed. Stripped of its usual careless charm and fixed in a grimace of bottomless rage. Lips bloodless slits, eyes narrowed with concentrated hatred. The ancient swords hung in a trembling, deadly semi-circle around the king for several terrible seconds that seemed to last a lifetime. Francis faced his own imminent demise with what could pass for relief. Theda cast a despairing glance at the

King, who nodded to his soldiers, and struggled to control her panic as the obedient guards drew their swords and marched forward.

"Sire, no, he would never harm you! You must believe me!"

She snatched at Robert's sleeve. Arm rigid as iron beneath her clawing fingers, his magic crackling around him, he ignored her. *"Robert, do not do this! You must stop!"* She shook him and increased the volume of her thoughts to a deafening level. Apart from a slight wince, he barely moved. Concentrating on the thin figure sitting rigidly on the throne, Robert appeared unaware of the guards as they encircled him in their own ring of steel. Powerful arms elbowed her roughly away.

"Robert, please!" Her cry of despair echoed from the walls of the chamber, and she shoved past a guard to reach him. Even without her staff, Mage power roared in her head, rippling through her hair and under her skin. Never had the battle to contain it taken so much of her self-control. The temptation to raze the throne room and wipe the smug expression from Darius's youthful face swept through her. Every dream and nightmare that had plagued her night-time rest over the last few years returned to flicker behind her eyes. Robert swayed when she flung both arms around him, enveloping him in her own power and draining some of his. He shuddered in her embrace, and she buried her head in his tobacco-scented robes as he dropped his weapons to the tiled floor with a clang like a thousand kettles. He drew her against his heart.

"Theda, I'm sorry, so sorry." His voice was a cracked whisper against her ear. "Please forgive me."

Speechless with terror, her arms tightened around him. Pressed hard against his chest, his heartbeat drummed panic in her ear.

"I don't know why you are waiting," Darius said to the guards, his voice as harsh as crows. Theda raised her tear-streaked gaze to where he stood, standing tall and straight at the King's side. A pillar of respectability in his obsidian black tunic and hose. His ermine cloak, the gold badge of rank gleaming dully in the wan light. Only his hat, the favourite red velvet she remembered from so many months ago, remained to remind her of the studious youth of old. A secretive gleam lit the inky depths of his eyes, a reptilian certainty that sent an icy shiver of distaste between her shoulders.

King Francis slumped on the throne at his side; he cut a vulnerable, frail figure. Even as she watched, Francis gathered himself to a more commanding stance against his cushions. Sorrow haunted his face as he waved a hand at the captain of the guard. Theda's gaze turned once more to his ring-bearing hand, and the dull light of the diamond that had once flashed with Eperan fire. Now, no more.

"The law is clear. The sentence is death," he said.

"No. This is wrong." She tore herself away from Robert's embrace and stumbled to her knees before the throne. "Your Majesty, I beg of you, do not do this. Show mercy."

Remote and powerful as the sun, Francis glared at her from under lowered brows. "You know our laws, Mistress. As do the Skinner family. Do not add yourself to the list of dissenters. It could go harsh with you."

"Theda, my love, do not risk yourself for me. The survival of magic in Epera rests with you."

Robert's voice in her head held a note of soul-wrenching sadness. She jerked her head around to look at him. Four soldiers held him in a grip of iron.

"This cannot be, Robert. Please, I must... let me..." She hardly knew what she asked of him. He shook his head, staring at Darius, icily remote.

"It is too late for me now. There is no way back from this. They want to make an example of the Blessed who defy the new orders. I am obviously

the chosen target, and like a fool, I stepped willingly into the trap they set when they took my son."

"Robert..."

At last, he looked at her. She locked her gaze on his, her cheeks wet with tears, petrified with fear for him. The guard dragged his arms behind him and wound a chain around his long, finely made hands. Robert flinched as the iron links bruised his wrists.

"I have always loved you, Theda. Since the first time I laid eyes on you. Pray for me, my dear."

"Please, your Majesty, reconsider. Do not do this, I beg of you!" She scrambled towards Francis, who still sat like a living skeleton against his cushions. Darius swept his sword from its scabbard, and she blinked as it whistled through the air to graze her throat.

"You do not approach His Majesty. Back away on your knees and let justice be served."

Theda ground her jaw and levered herself from the cold marble floor to look him straight in the eye. The power of the Mage rippled around her to raise her hair, and she took a slim draught of comfort from the warmth of her God's presence, even if she dared not trust herself to use his power.

Brow furrowing with suspicion, Darius took an almost imperceptible step back in the face of her wrath.

"This is not justice," she snapped, bitterness in every syllable. "This is murder."

The King's Guard hanged Robert less than two hours later from a makeshift gibbet erected in haste in the central courtyard. Stunned into horrified silence, the entire population of the Castle of Air crammed into the vast space, ringed about by iron-faced guards gripping unsheathed swords. King Francis watched from a narrow balcony, with Darius on one side of him and Dupliss on the other. Still clad in her court gown, Theda trembled with shock and rage at the front of the crowd. Briana was nowhere to be seen. She must have taken refuge in the Queen's apartments, her household the only members of the Court not commanded to attend. The soft afternoon light leant a warm autumnal glow to the scene, painting it in a sympathetic light it did not deserve. A chill wind fluttered the pennants, and a single drum beat marked Robert's footsteps as he walked to his doom. The rough rope of the gibbet swayed gently in the breeze. Waiting.

Bruises and blood marked his skin, but he seemed unaware of the discomfort. White faced, Robert stared up at the sky, at the castle starlings as they wheeled and called above his head. The guards had taken care to keep his hands bound. The clink of the heavy iron as he mounted the platform echoed from the walls. Theda opened her mental channels to their fullest extent. All she found was emptiness. Robert had tamped down his power, and the telepathic members of the castle had left weeks before. She could have called him. Every particle of her demanded a last conversation, yearned to hear his laughing voice in her head just one more time. Nothing. Swallowing, she reined in her own wants, cursing her own selfishness. Unbidden, her hands curled into fists. Sharp nails dug into her palms, whilst guilt and anger at her own inaction battled within her heart. What was the use of it? This God-given power she could not use in defence of injustice without risking its loss. This constant struggle as a Seer to remain impartial when the human part of her wanted to scream at the heavens and raze the castle and all its inhabitants to dust.

Robert took the last few steps to the rope, and Theda bit her lip until it bled, swiping at the tears that stung her eyes and blurred her vision. At the least, she had to bear witness. It was the only thing she could do.

The captain of the King's Guard stepped forward, face a blank mask, and tightened the noose around Robert's neck. The drumbeat stopped. Robert waited, his eyes still fixed on the starlings. The guard stepped back and let his cold blue gaze wander across the throng.

"Hear ye. This man, Robert Skinner, attempted to murder the King with his Blessed gift. Watch and know the penalty in Epera for treason." His parade ground voice blared across the courtyard and echoed from the walls. The crowd gasped. Somewhere, a child cried. The guard nodded to his second, who laid a leather-gloved hand on the lever that would open the platform under Robert's softly shod feet and break his neck.

The drumbeat started again.

One.

"I love you, Robert. I should have told you. Why didn't I tell you?"

Two.

"No. No. Please, my love...wait. Stop. Don't leave me."

Three.

Robert's gaze dropped to hers.

"Save the magic, my love."

And then the platform snapped open beneath him, and he was gone.

Chapter Twenty-Three

From the journal of Briana of the Owls, September 1569

It has been a week and I have not seen her. Of all my mother's visions since I arrived, this had to be the one that she saw true. I should have listened to her. Trusted her. She has done all she can for me, and Epera and its magic, with no thanks and no reward. When the power of the Dark Mage leaves me, I can see her just as she is, a powerful woman who will turn to no-one for comfort in her days of grief. I've done so many terrible things to harm her, and when I tried to call our wedding off one more time, Darius stood in front of me, with his hands on his hips and told me he suspects her of being one of the Blessed. He said she would follow Robert Skinner to the gallows unless I became his wife.

So I'm sorry, my dear mother. I have no choice. This time, I must defy you to save you. I must marry this monster. It's what I deserve. Gods forgive me. I know you will never want to speak to me again.

Days passed, and Theda sat unmoving in her chair in front of the fire, staring at nothing in the leaping flames. Thin fingers cradled Robert's long clay pipe in her lap, its shallow bowl rubbed smooth with time and use. Scattered crumbs and spilt wine littered the surface of the table, drawn up beside her. Ever faithful, Jacklyn arrived twice every day, offering food and drink. She took the wine. It passed her lips with ease. A memory of happier days blunted the devastation playing inside her angry, broken heart. She had yet to change from her crumpled court gown, the bodice now blotched with sweat, tears, and drink stains like dried blood. Food was unthinkable. Sleep impossible.

"Won't you take something to eat, Mistress?" Jacklyn said on the evening of the sixth day. He crouched in front of her to capture her absent attention. One gentle, giant hand landed on her arm. She glanced down at the squared-off nails and the wiry dark hair that sprinkled its back and then returned her gaze to the fire. A hundred different scenes drifted through her tired mind, recalling another time and another slender, more elegant hand with the power to move the world. Tears stung her eyes, and she let go of Robert's pipe only long enough to swipe them away.

"I do not wish for food."

Jacklyn sighed and eased himself upright, dusting stale breadcrumbs from the table to the grubby floor.

"I will send a chamberer to you, Mistress. Tis not right you should rot in here by yourself, surrounded by rubbish. Where is Briana? Surely you wish to see your daughter on the eve of her wedding?"

"No." Her voice emerged harsh as rust with disuse, sharper than she had intended.

She glanced up at Jacklyn as he scrubbed a hand through his unruly hair, a perplexed frown creasing his youthful forehead. Confusion and despair haunted his expression. She could almost trace the thoughts that crossed his mind. Worry for her. Pride in his work for the Mage and the transportation of the magical collection. And the constant question that haunted every member of the population in the days since the closing of the temples. How long will this last? Surely everything will go back to normal soon.

She cleared her throat, a bitter smile tugging at the corners of her mouth.

"Nothing will change, Jacklyn. Not for a long time."

He startled. "How did you know what I was thinking?"

Tired to her soul, she managed a shrug. "Change is hard to accept for all of us. Your wants are mine, lad. But there is no going back from this. We must accept it. Do our best, I suppose."

Jacklyn poured them both some ale and slumped into the seat opposite, keeping a wary eye on the closed door.

"The books are safe, Mistress," he assured her in a low voice. "At least for now. What do you want me to do with them? My father says our team is too scared to enter the storeroom."

Her lips twisted in a semblance of a smile. "Yes, the books and artefacts are overwhelming in a small space, especially for those with any type of magical gift. I'm guessing one of your father's group is a latent telepath if he senses their power."

Jacklyn's chin jerked an acknowledgement. "My brother, Dunstan. He's fifteen. He was going to study under Master Skinner, but..."

He stopped, dark eyes flying to hers as he realised his error.

Theda pressed her tankard hard against her chest at the mention of Robert's name and forced herself to consider his question. "I will leave this castle at some point, Jacklyn. If your father will grant me a little more time, tell him the collection will go with me to the Mage Tree in Goldfern Woods. It is accessible by boat down the Cryfell. I will require a team of powerful men and the utmost secrecy. But I'm sure he will arrange that."

He nodded. "As you wish, Mistress. 'T'is just Dunstan. He enjoys scaring his friends."

Her eyebrows quirked. "I hope he also understands how precious that collection is. Can he trust these friends of his? What if one of them is an informer? What if someone tells a member of the King's Guard about his undisclosed Blessed status?"

Jacklyn bristled. "We are all loyal to the Mage, Mistress. And to each other."

Theda shrugged. "Yes, well. Warn him, anyway. We think the rules are harsh now, but the Gods know it will get worse yet. I'd hate your brother to share the same fate as Terrence Skinner."

The young man blanched. "I will do that. About Briana, are you certain you will not see the maid? I escorted the Queen's women to supper yester eve, and she looks just as bad as you."

Theda lowered her drink and turned Robert's pipe once more in her hand. She scowled at him. "Is that what you are here for, Jacklyn? To petition me on behalf of my daughter?"

"Nay, nay!" Jacklyn's face creased in alarm at the thought. "But they are busy even now in the Great Hall, preparing for the morrow. The Queen is all pins and needles about the arrangements, and Briana... Well, she looks so lost. Scared. I'd have to have a heart of stone not to be worried for her. She needs her ma, to my way of thinking. Not that old battle-axe of a Queen Mother."

Theda's lips thinned. "She's marrying my Lord Falconridge of her own free will. It is a dark path, and I have always warned her against it. But she chose not to listen. I can't think what comfort I can bring her now."

Jacklyn reached for the poker and leaned forward to prod the coals to a better life. “She’s your daughter, mistress,” he said.

Theda turned her gaze once more to the crackling blaze, her face a mask of bitterness.

“She has betrayed me,” she said.

“Nay, never her. Surely you do not think it?” The young soldier’s face turned white. “Briana would not do that. Could not do that.”

“You really think so, Jacklyn? When you know as well as I what we have seen play out beneath our own eyes? That lad she is marrying will be the death of her. She’s a fool. A lovesick, besotted fool who did not abide my warnings and is now wearing some trinket that seeks to ensnare her soul. What am I supposed to think? She has made her choice. She’s chosen to marry the man who ordered the death of someone powerful and good. Someone I loved.” Her voice broke in a crack of grief, and Jacklyn flinched as she hurled her tankard at the cold stone wall. Pale ale dripped like tears towards the hearth.

Jacklyn swallowed as the curtains swelled in a Mage-born wind. “I beg you, Mistress, think of what the Mage might want in all this,” he urged.

“The Mage.” Theda’s teeth bared in a bitter snarl. “All my life, I have sought to understand his messages. I have trodden his path at his behest. My task is to protect this kingdom, its population, and its magic. And look. Look what has become of it under my service. The temples closed. Our Blessed population rounded up to slave in the mines. Dear Robert, dead. My daughter, lost to me.” She scrabbled for her staff, where it lay by her chair, and Jacklyn jumped to his feet with a yell of dismay as she hefted it from the floor and thrust it into the flames.

"This for the Mage," she hissed. "I am expected to stand by and watch while these atrocities play out. I am done. He has taken everything from me and left us with nothing."

Boosted by magic, the weak fire flared with the strength of ten of its kind. Flames roared up the ancient chimney and leapt from the tiny hearth to torch the hem of Theda's gown. With a yelp of alarm, Jacklyn snatched the precious wood from the blaze. Theda sat, immobile, ready for the flames to take her, but the fireplace settled to comfortable peace as soon as the staff lay safe in the soldier's hands. Jacklyn stamped out her skirts and surveyed his prize with astonishment. A coil of white smoke curled around its handle. The carving of the Mage Tree gleamed with health as it always had, no worse for its encounter with the element of fire. His hand shook as he laid it with careful reverence across Theda's soiled lap and folded her stiff hands around it.

"This is yours, Mistress," he said, his voice rough and stern. "And the Mage himself has trusted you with it all this long time. Will you let him down now? When he needs you? Maybe this is your test, Mistress. Did you ever think about that?"

Theda stared numbly at the ancient stave that lay across her knees alongside Robert's pipe. In her head, the Mage's challenge from all those months ago whispered once more, soft as autumn leaves. "What will you give to save the future?"

Eyes stinging with smoke, she raised her head to meet Jacklyn's steadfast dark eyes as he towered over her.

"The Mage is blessed to have you serve him. In a time of great trial, your faith is greater than mine," she said.

Jacklyn's firm lips twitched in a tiny smile as he glanced once more around the room for anything else that may have caught fire. "I'm a simple soldier, Mistress. Not a Seer. Not Blessed. My only responsibility is to obey orders, not talk to a God. We all do our duty. And just now, my duty is to serve the Mage and you."

Her head dipped in acknowledgement. A gentle thrum of power warmed her fingers where they lay against the twisted wood, and, for the first time in days, some small comfort bled from the staff to ease her aching heart. She bent over it, cradling it to her.

Jacklyn stood back. "If you will, Mistress, I will send a chamberer to you. There's a bonny lass in the maid's quarters at a loose end just now since her patron left for her estate. She'll look after ye. Fetch ye a bath and food. Clean the place."

Theda glanced around at her filthy quarters and wrinkled skirts as if seeing them for the first time and then laid Robert's pipe gently in the saucer at her side.

"My thanks, Jacklyn. For all you have done."

He smiled at her, relief etched across his face. "'T'is no bother. I'll fetch Dora."

He left the room, letting the door close behind him with a gentle click. Alone once more, Theda straightened her back and used the staff to ease herself to her feet. Her legs wobbled under her, but she staggered to the window and leaned her head against the panes to stare at the rising moon. Unbidden, a memory of another evening like this one tickled the back of her mind. For a moment, she could swear Robert Skinner stood behind her, his lightly bearded chin resting on the top of her head, his arms holding her close against his heart. Her eyes closed. The subtle smell of Argent Gold rose to tease her nostrils.

"Robert," she whispered deep inside her mind.

And his answering whisper, softer than the sigh of a starling's wing. *"Save the magic, my love."*

Chapter Twenty-Four

Briana of the Owls on the eve of her wedding.

I'm writing this now as a record before I lose my freedom or the Shadow Mage battles for my mind again. Either way, I'm as good as dead.

Ariana has spared no expense from the Queen's purse to dress me like a princess. These are real clothes. Not my normal day dress, veiled with illusion. It's heavy, this concoction of brocade and velvet. Ariana commanded her dressmakers to construct a square-necked gown cut too low for my liking. It's embroidered with falcons and owls in brown and blue, picked out in gold thread. Magnificent. As befits the new Lady of Falconridge. Darius sent me his mother's coronet and jewels this morning. He didn't appear in person, of course. He knows I have no desire for this marriage. There was a note instructing me to wear the jewels in honour of his family. The House of the Falcon is rich indeed. They nest their diamonds in storm grey and sky blue. Stunning, intricate, and surpassingly graceful settings that remind me of swooping wings. Light and freedom. I had to close the box. It is so ironic that I will wear these precious objects and be bound forever in the grip of the Shadow Mage and a tyrant who would take that power for his own if he could. I wish my mother was here. Gods know, I need her wisdom now. She must think I have forsaken her. My actions will appear wilful and vain. Marriage to

Darius will be hard. I know that. With luck, his court business will take him far from Falconridge. Perhaps it will be possible to make a life in the wilderness of the northern ranges, high in the hills where the falcons fly. I must think that. Otherwise, the thought of what I am about to do will drive me mad.

"I've done my best, Mistress Eglion, but some of these stains are impossible."

In the chill light of the late autumn morning, Theda shivered in her shift in front of the banked fireplace. A hard frost had gripped the castle overnight, and Jacklyn was yet to arrive with her daily supply of coal. The old blue gown was indeed a sorry state. Still damp from Dora's hasty ministrations and heavy with the dreadful memories of the previous week's events, it lay like a ragged corpse in the maid's arms. Her jaw tightened as she looked at it. Court gown or not, she never wanted to see it again.

"Salvage any part of that for your own use, my dear. I'll wear the black. It's in my trunk," she said, rubbing at the gooseflesh that pimpled her arms.

"At a wedding?"

"At this wedding, it's the best possible colour. Believe me," Theda said.

Her new maid shook her head, but she crossed into the bedchamber and returned with the decorous ink hued robe Theda had always felt most comfortable in. Dora tightened the laces as far as they would go and made quick work of attaching the dull sleeves. Folded within its warmth, Theda picked at the food Dora had brought her and tried to smooth her hair into order.

A rattle of bucket and a brief tap on the outer door signalled Jacklyn's arrival. He strode in at her call to enter, nodding approval at the newly freshened chamber.

"There, Mistress. I told ye our Dora would do a good job," he declared, setting the bucket down with a clang and putting the fire to rights.

"Aw, you big lummox. Did you truly say that?" The maid's eyes sparked with affection as she bustled to the window and busied herself arranging the drapes. A light blush stained her cheeks. Her suitor braced his hands on his knees and gave her a warm look that bespoke his adoration.

"Aye, my rose, and quite right, too. Credit where it's due and all that." He stood up and glanced down at Theda's empty plate with a satisfied glint in his eye. "How are you feeling, Mistress? Better this morning, I hope?"

Theda's heart lurched in her chest. Somehow, overnight, she had wrestled her grief into a cage within her mind. Robert's ghost roamed its perimeter, accompanied by the aroma of Argent Gold. She'd lain awake much of the night, thinking about Jacklyn's words. There was little she could find to reject them. Even in his youth, the young man's sturdy sense of duty and loyalty bumped against her sense of betrayal and outrage. The way of the Seer. A lonely path, always. That much she had always known. Farsight had its price, after all. Nothing was ever gained without substantial cost. Robert's lively presence had reminded her of happier days of love and courtship before the mantle of the Seer fell to her on the death of her beloved husband. She'd taken the burden gladly then. Seen it as a symbol of the Mage's faith in her. It had been a comfort. A blessing. Would she reject it now?

No.

"I will always be grateful for your care of me, Jacklyn Sommerton," she said into the awkward silence that had fallen between them. "You reminded me of my duty. I needed to hear it."

He shuffled his feet. "Aye, well," he muttered. Hands like shovels fluttered at his sides, looking for something to do, and she shook her head at his embarrassment.

"Credit where it's due and all that," she said with light irony.

He chuckled and strode over to the window embrasure to pull his lady into a warm embrace. "There, my rose, that'll have to do for now. I'm to report to duty in the King's guard this morning."

Dora batted his arms away. "Get away with you. I'll have to get on, too, now. I'm standing in for one of the other maids this morn." She bobbed a quick curtsey to Theda. "'T'was a pleasure serving you, Mistress," she said.

"Thank you, Dora." Theda blinked at the pair of them surrounded by the morning light and smiled at the strongest image the Mage showed her. "My blessing on your marriage," she murmured.

Dora's blue eyes rounded with surprise, her ready blush once more staining her cheeks. Theda could see why, to Jacklyn, the girl was his rose.

"Mistress?" Jacklyn's deep voice asked for reassurance, and she raised her head to nod at him.

"The Mage wills your happiness and will not forget your service. Your part in this story is not yet done."

To her surprise, they knelt in front of her and joined hands, as engaged couples in the Temple of the Mage would have done before

Darius disbanded the clergy. She raised her hand in blessing and waited as they regained their feet, their youthful faces solemn with purpose.

At the door, Dora turned to smile, and Theda's spirits lifted a small degree. "Don't forget the velvet," she said.

"Are you sure? 'T'is not servant's garb."

"Who says you will always be a servant? Take it."

They left her, Dora's arms full of expensive material. Theda's lips thinned as the door closed behind them. There was another wedding in the more immediate future, and Jacklyn was right. Briana needed her more than ever.

Leaving the privacy of her rooms to join the bustle of the wider castle shocked her raw senses. With a noble wedding taking place, the castle seemed full to bursting. Theda hurried along to the Queen's apartments with a flask of cold heartsease tea clamped to her ribs under her bodice. Citizens of every stripe and order crowded the passageways. The air buzzed alive with the hum of conversation. The Blessed were nowhere to be seen. In the last week, since the death of one of their most illustrious fellows, the remaining members of the Blessed population had taken fright and left. Theda bit her lip as she scanned the crowd. Distance muted even the Lord Chamberlain, Sir Walter Smythe's mental signature. He'd clearly fled as well. She wondered briefly who had taken his place. Another one of Darius's picks, probably. In their absence, the population of the Castle of Air comprised many fresh faces. Newly made knights and baronets, ambitious merchants and artisans had taken over, confident in their new status.

As she approached, the King's guard standing to attention outside the Queen's apartments nodded in recognition. She waited as he stepped inside to announce her and stiffened her shoulders. Hard to know what she would face. The gleeful face of the Shadow Mage or her vulnerable daughter.

Eager not to arouse the wrath of the Queen, Theda was ready with her full court curtsey as a page announced her into Ariana's outer chamber. The mound of grey velvet she'd most recently seen piled on the floor now framed the view from the sunlit windows. Ariana's stomach blossomed. In the last few months of her pregnancy, her skin glowed rich cream, her blonde hair glossy with health. At her side, dressed in her favourite purple, Theodora placed her hands on her ample hips and raised her eyebrows.

"Mistress Eglion, how nice to see you again, although I am surprised to see you up and about. We were told you were ill."

As ever, Theda shielded her thoughts from the woman's telepathic curiosity. "I have been ill," she said, "but I am much recovered and eager to see my daughter. Is she here?"

Ariana's smooth brow quirked. "She sent word out that she is ill as well. Her maid said she has lost a lot of weight this last week, and we have had to alter her gown, but she is in her room. Are you sure you are well?" The Queen's jewelled hand strayed protectively to the mound of her belly.

"Nothing contagious, Madam, I assure you," Theda said, foot tapping under her cloak. "May I go to Briana?"

The royal women exchanged glances. "I suppose we can allow it," Ariana said. "My mother attended me before my marriage to the King. But do not tarry. We are due downstairs at noon."

Theda dipped her head, and the Wessendeans parted to give access to a door on the far side of the chamber. Hurrying through it, she found herself in an adjoining, lamp-lit corridor leading to a smaller set of rooms with less embellishment decorating the pale oak frames.

"Briana?"

Silence. Should she open her mental channels? What would the Shadow Mage do if he was lurking at the surface of Briana's thoughts right now? She dared not risk it. Taking a deep breath, summoning strength from the Mage to protect her, she cracked open the nearest door.

Dressed in a simple shift, Briana stood at her window. At her side, a sullen servant waited. Her arms laboured under the weight of the rich brocade that draped them. The simple, four-poster bed was a mess of tossed pillows and tumbled blankets. An uneaten breakfast balanced precariously on the edge of a small side table. A small chest, embellished with the emblem of the Falcons, waited on Briana's dressing table.

"Come, your ladyship, it's time to dress. You've been stood there all morning. Do you hear me?"

The woman's impatient tone showed this was not the first time she'd uttered this sentence. Theda's brow contracted as the woman took a step forward and poked her daughter hard in the ribs. Fury bloomed somewhere near her frozen heart.

"You may leave us," she said sharply from the door.

The attendant jumped, suspicion written across her face. "Who are you?"

"I am her ladyship's mother, and if that is the best of your service, you are clearly in the wrong occupation." Theda strode to her daughter and reached a gentle hand to turn her around. Briana resisted her effort. Her entire body trembled with tension.

"It's not my fault," the maid grumbled. "Queen sent me to dress her, and she won't move. Been stood here since first light, I have."

"Get out."

"But..."

A snarl twisting her lips, Theda rounded on her and pointed at the door. "Go. I will see to my daughter's welfare since you cannot."

The attendant shrugged and dropped the dress on the bed. "On your head it'll be if she's late," she prophesied gloomily. "Don't say I didn't warn ye."

She sneered at Theda's narrowed expression and sauntered to the door, insolence in every line of her. "Shoes are under the bed, jewels in that there chest. Good luck."

Theda's nails clawed her palms. *"Just a little telekinesis,"* she begged the Mage, struggling to keep her temper in check. *"Just enough to smack her in the back of her head with a hairbrush on her way out."*

The door snicked shut, and at last, Theda could stand in front of Briana and take her measure.

"Briana?"

Nothing. Up close, sweat bloomed on the girl's forehead, her breath light and panting. At her side, dainty palms clenched into fists. Her betrothal ring dug deep into her finger. The surrounding flesh stood proud and swollen. Theda waved a hand in front of her face. Briana didn't blink. Her grey eyes were fixed on World's Peak, home to the Gods, far away to the south. Straining her magical senses, Theda caught the whisper of Briana's mental voice, growing louder as her control over her defences slipped.

"Mage, help me. Gods help me. Keep me strong. Keep it out, I beg you. By all the Gods, Mage, help me..."

Prayer. Theda's heart collapsed in her chest, and she regarded her daughter with horror. Ariana had not understated the need for alteration of the wedding gown. Briana's cheekbones jutted, the fine skin stretched over them grey with dehydration. How long had she shut herself away to battle the Shadow Mage whilst Theda kept to her room and indulged her grief?

Self-disgust gnawed at her as she drew the potion from its hiding place and uncorked the flask. Briana's nose wrinkled at the bittersweet aroma, and Theda waved it under her chin, hoping the scent would smooth the way.

"Briana, my dear one, take some of this. It will help you hold him off, I promise, just for a little while." She inched the flask closer, tipped a little over her palm, and touched the liquid to Briana's parched lips. Dehydration won the day for her. Briana's tongue crept out instinctively to taste the water. Encouraged, Theda swiped a cup from the breakfast table, threw the contents into the empty chamber pot and filled it with the remains of the flask. Desperate for liquid, Briana drank.

Theda was ready when Briana dropped into her arms like a stone. As weak as each other, they staggered to the bed. Theda smoothed her daughter's hair as Briana's bleary gaze focused on her surroundings.

"Mother?"

"I'm here."

"Has it gone?"

Theda grimaced. "I'm afraid not, my dear. There was not enough in that flask to banish him for more than a few hours. Perhaps you feel calmer, though?"

"I hate it. I hate myself, mother. Please help me. This is all my fault. Robert Skinner. Terrence..."

Theda hugged her, cradling the rumpled head against her shoulder.

"It is not your fault, Briana. You were not to know any of this would happen. If anyone is to blame, it is I. The Mage has shown me much of what is coming to pass, and I, in my pride and fear for the future, did not want to believe it."

"I should have listened to you. Why didn't I listen to your warnings?"

"Hush now. It's not too late. We can call it off, you don't have..."

Even as she began the sentence, her attention snared on the silver gilt of the large mirror standing proud on Briana's dressing table. Eyes wide, she stared at their reflection, curled together on the bed as the rest of the room smudged into shadows.

"You don't understand. I've done something... Mother?"

The reflection blurred, and she blinked; refocused as Briana's voice faded. An unfamiliar woman looked back at her. Thin; her long dark hair prematurely lit with strands of silver. Dark blue eyes, solemn and deep as the midnight sky. As Theda looked, the woman glanced down, turning her hand to observe the dull diamond ring that weighed so heavily on her finger. The Ring of Mercy. A Queen, then. One not yet born.

Even from this distance, Theda could sense her latent power. Her sadness and confusion. The desperate loneliness of her heart. The family bonds.

"Mother?"

She coughed, dragged her eyes away from the mirror and returned her attention to the girl who lay so terrified in her arms.

"I have to marry him, mother." Briana's voice was dull with regret.

Theda glanced up at the mirror once more, but the Mage's vision had passed. The mirror showed nothing more than her daughter, a young woman, shivering in a thin silk shift, and herself, an ageing crone dressed entirely in black.

She sighed. This time she wouldn't obfuscate. Wouldn't question the vision of the Mage. It had been clear enough, even for her.

She tightened her arms, her heart heavy with resignation. This was the price the Mage demanded of her to save the future.

"Yes, my dear. I'm afraid you do."

Chapter Twenty-Five

Seated somewhere in the middle of the Great Hall, surrounded by gossiping Citizens clad in newly bought finery, Theda's nails dug into her perspiring palms. Jaw clenched, she scanned the room, trying to ignore the clutching dread that clamped her belly. Ariana's plans for this wedding eclipsed even her mother's vision for the feast on the eve of Darius's preferment. The servants had stacked the boards against the walls and placed the usual benches in rows facing the king's dais. Garlanded with autumn blooms, the platform waited for the ceremony that would join Briana to Darius. Owls to Falcons. Two noble houses entwined forever. Long strips of material painted with images of leaves in copper and russet swathed the ancient beams. The looping lengths created the illusion of a tented, intimate space. Images of Owls and Falcons fluttered against the tall walls, floating gently in the chill breeze from the cracked open windows. Theda inhaled the essence of fallen leaves and wood smoke underlaid with the promise of ice and winterberries. Hundreds of candles, now painstakingly lit by hand in the absence of Robert's talent, added a flickering glow to the scene. Girdred had composed a suite of new airs for the occasion, and his tuneful tenor weaved a thread of delicate melody under the din of chatter.

Unthinking, one of her hands crept from her lap, seeking the solace of Robert's warm fingers. A rough clearing of the throat jerked her back to reality, and she snatched her fingers away from the muscular thigh of an unfamiliar merchant. The man stared at her lustily from beneath the luxurious brocade of his hat, and she muttered an apology, her face burning.

The man laughed, and she caught the whiff of alcohol on his breath. "No need to apologise, Mistress. I am at your service," he said with a wink.

Theda ignored him, cloaking herself in silence, and opened her mental channels. If she could not be at her daughter's side as the girl walked the path to her dark future, she would at least give what comfort she could. Even if Briana dared not use her gift whilst under the possession of the Shadow Mage, perhaps she would still sense that her mother was there.

A blare of trumpets quieted the crowd as the king and the royal household entered. Along with everyone else, Theda rose to her feet, but she kept her gaze ahead, her hands clenched at her sides. No more would she bow to a monarch who had abandoned his faith and his people. Dupliss, clothed in rich shades of copper and green, obviously chosen by the Queen, followed the royal party. A light flush stained his sallow cheeks. Theda bit her lip on a laugh. Too much wine, or just embarrassment at the garishness of his attire? She'd never known Dupliss to wear anything other than serviceable black. Her shoulder blades tightened in anticipation as the King took his seat in the front row. Ariana lowered herself uncomfortably into her own chair, and the company rustled to the benches. Apart from the odd cough and sniffle, silence reigned.

At a nod from the King, Girdred took up his harp and raised his voice in song once more. The decorations rippled as the heavy doors opened, and Darius strode down the aisle to the raised stage. He'd left off his sombre attire for the occasion. Instead, his expensive doublet was a triumph of cut sleeves featuring sky-blue silk under a gleaming layer of charcoal brocade. His badge of rank dominated his broad chest; a jaunty falcon feather attached to his hat with a diamond cockade grazed his cheekbone. A long cloak fell in heavy folds to brush rushes from the stone flags. Despite the celebratory attire, the lad's expression wore an expression that combined equal parts fierce purpose and high-handed pride. Theda's lips tightened in a grim line as he passed her line of sight. She expected to see the dark presence following him, but this afternoon, Darius appeared purely himself, and she passed a hand over her brow to massage the frown there, wondering if Briana and Robert had both been correct all those months ago. Perhaps she had imagined it.

Darius mounted the low platform and clasped forearms in greeting with Dupliss, who managed a tight smile. Together, the two men turned to survey the hushed company, and then the doors opened once more to admit Briana, standing alone and vulnerable on the threshold.

The onlookers stood, and Girdred's voice swelled to a crescendo as she took her first hesitant steps forward. She stared ahead at nothing. Theda surveyed her anxiously as she whispered past, softly shod feet hushed as snowflakes against the rush-covered flags. The heavy cloak and train of her dress slowed her progress. Briana had almost closed her mental channels. Her face shone pale as the moon, shadowed by tension. Her hands twisted nervously around a bouquet of autumn roses, and the icy glint of diamonds shed their glittering light from her ears and throat.

At the platform, she curtsied to the King and Queen. Her eyes snapped into sudden, anxious focus as she rose, searching for Theda, cloaked in black. A shadow amongst a sea of colour on the crowded benches.

"My dearest daughter, have courage," Theda whispered to her through their mental connection. *"I understand you have your own reasons for this marriage, but all is not lost. Hard though it is to believe, your descendants will be the ones to bring this kingdom back to the Mage."*

"Truly, mother? The Mage trusts me still?"

Her daughter's mental voice appeared tiny. Conflicted and squeezed from behind the habitual guard she built around her thoughts. Theda placed her hand on her heart and dipped her head. *"We must trust the Mage, my dear, as he trusts in us. All else is illusion. You, of all his disciples, must know this by now."*

The first genuine smile in weeks lifted her lips as her daughter straightened her back and squared her shoulders. Eyes sparkling to match the diamonds she wore, Briana turned and stared straight at her. She placed her own hand on her heart and bowed her head. Around them, the company muttered in confusion at the small departure from their expectations. Hard eyes turned to Theda, where she sat in silent communion with her daughter. Moments passed. On the dais, Darius took a step forward, a suspicious frown plastered across his face, and Dupliss coughed to gain the bride's attention.

"We should get on." King Francis's querulous tones rang around the room.

"Your Majesty." Briana curtsied formally to the elderly monarch again. And she still smiled, one copper eyebrow quirked in a sarcastic question as she ascended the platform and extended her hand to Darius.

"My Lord," she said, "Shall we wed?"

Chapter Twenty-Six

The feasting that accompanied the wedding celebrations lasted long into the evening. Everyone, it seemed, wished to congratulate the newly wedded couple. An army of servants appeared seconds after the service to transform the room from ceremonial space to banquet hall, and the castle kitchen staff bustled forth with all the bounty of the autumn season, seasoned with precious spices and washed down with vintage wine. Theda ate sparingly and caught her daughter's eye as she prepared to leave the room. Briana cut a fragile figure at the top table, flanked by her husband on the one side and Dupliss on the other. Despite the rising hope budding in her chest, Theda couldn't help but shudder at the sight of her slim daughter hemmed and hedged in her new status by the dominant men who would now control her future. With the assurance that her God still had a use for her, Briana played her part well. The heartsease tea Theda had encouraged her to drink tempered her magic for now and thus the hold of the Shadow Mage, although for how much longer, she could not tell. From a distance, Briana appeared much the same vivacious girl who had charmed her way into Francis's new inner circle all those many months ago.

"Meet me in the library later," Theda told her as she left the rowdy party for the peace of her own chambers. *"Don't get drunk. We have work to do, you and I."*

"What work?" Briana asked, lowering her goblet for a moment.

"I will tell you later."

"I can't. This is my wedding night. I think I am expected somewhere else."

Briana's mental voice was flippant, and Theda frowned. *"Get him drunk. If you can. But you must meet me. Tonight. In the library."*

"I don't think so. I know you, old woman. You have a plan."

On her way through the door, Theda shuddered at the malicious voice in her head and shut her mental channels with a ferocity that made her muscles jerk in response. Heart twisting in defeat, she glanced back at Briana. Surrounded by drunk, cavorting citizens, the girl raised her glass in an ironic salute. Darkness sparked in the depths of her crystal eyes. Theda swallowed and turned away, her heart grim with foreboding. The draft of heartsease tea taken hours before had worn off, and Briana had exhausted her own mental resources. Her magic roared for release, and the Shadow Mage was back.

Lips compressed to a thin, hard line, Theda climbed the stairs to her apartment as fast as she could, struggling to control her panic. Her chambers lay cold and damp, and she closed the window against the chilly night air before turning to her trunk. Scattering the contents onto her bed, her hands closed on the only magical book left of the collection. Heaving it into the dim light, she sat with it for a moment on her lap, stroking its familiar, thick vellum pages. Her own book of shadows, handed down to her from the previous Seer as tradition dictated, along with her staff. Of all the books in the magical collection, this was the most powerful, comprehensive volume of Eperan magic in existence. It was the only artefact she could leave for her future descendent to find. It contained much that a person new to magic would need to know. But how could she secure its safety for the years that would follow as the population of Epera continued to deny the Mage? The Queen's rooms were out of the question. Heavily guarded and regularly cleaned. Chewing her lip as she considered the problem, she retrieved her staff from its hiding place and placed the book in a satchel under her voluminous cloak. Cocking her head at an inner prompting, she brewed a strong solution of heartsease tea, decanted it into a corked flask and added it to the load. Taking one long look around her sanctuary, she lifted her shoulders in a shrug. There was only one place that made sense.

The ancient library lay hushed as a tomb, far from the rowdiness of the feasting courtiers. Shutting the heavy door, Theda reached for the heavy lantern kept on the shelf and fumbled in the folds of her cloak for her flint. Not for the first time, she missed Robert's obliging gift of light as she struck a spark and held it to the wick.

The lantern flared to life, and she lifted it, breathing in the familiar smell of vellum, dust, and ink. Even in silence, the space seemed filled with the murmur of distant conversation, with bursts of laughter or academic argument, the treble chatter of children. And Robert. Dear Robert. She started forward; the satchel bumping heavy against her narrow haunches, weighing her down. The lamp light flickered, highlighting the shelves one at a time as she passed. She'd not returned since Skinner's arrest. Piles of paper from the ruined books still lay in orderly rows from the night they had spent trying to sort them out, arguing about how to approach the King, their mood veering from optimism to anger and back. Chairs stood where the students had left them, hastily scraped away from the battered tables, their quills drying in their empty inkwells, leaving essays and treatises half finished. She bit her lip, stifling a sob with an effort, trying to keep her mind on the task ahead. Where could she leave the book where no one would find it? She'd had the idea of hiding it in plain sight, but there was no guarantee that some enthusiastic scholar would not stumble across it. And if they were a Citizen steeped in zealotry? Enemies of Magic?

They'd destroy the book. Then all hope for Epera would die, withered on the vine. She couldn't risk it. The Restricted section? But that was empty now. And how would she guide a future person to the key?

Heaving a sigh, she stopped where she was and held up the lantern. Shelf number seventy-six. The history section. Most of its contents seemed intact. She took a few long steps into the narrow space between the rows and placed the lamp carefully on a hook designed for the purpose. If ever there was a time to trust the Mage, this was it.

Never one for ritual, Theda shrugged the heavy bag from her shoulders and heaved the book onto the nearest shelf. Centring herself, shutting her eyes, she braced her staff before her and called for the power of the Mage. It sang through her staff into her hands, and she placed one on the worn cover. *"Mage take you and cover you,"* she urged, willing her magic into the ancient pages. *"Conceal you until the next Seer comes."* Mage wind billowed around her, lifting her cloak and her hair from its untidy coil. Her palms itched with power as it poured into the book, but even with the amplification of the staff, the ancient tome resisted her efforts.

"Disappear," she begged it. *"Please, for the good of Epera. For the Blessing of Magic in the future. Conceal yourself."* Her heart raced as she pushed her will into the future. *"Conceal yourself now and until the next Seer comes."*

The book flickered and vanished. The air around it felt warm. Scorched. She'd just taken a well-earned breath, congratulating herself, when it reappeared.

"By the Gods."

Overwhelmed with exhaustion at the huge call on her magical resources, she slumped against the stack, heart and head pounding in double time. The book lay silent and massively real on its oak bed. Theda scowled at it for a moment, and then her head slumped against her chest. What was the use? This was not her gift. She needed Briana. And the Shadow Mage controlled her. It was over. There was nothing more she could do. She'd just have to leave it. Take the risk.

Bracing herself against her staff, she levered herself to her feet while the headache corkscrewed into the narrow space between her eyes. Chewing her lips, she spent a few moments crowding the volume around with the most obscure titles she could see. Standing back to survey her handiwork, she shook her head in frustration. Ancient and complex as it was, the Book of Shadows was clearly different from the surrounding items. Older. Handbound. Intriguing. It commanded attention. Nothing retiring about it at all.

She heaved a sigh, her mouth screwed into a grimace of frustration. What next? If that didn't work, what else could she do?

"Mother?"

Theda jumped, eyes darting around the small pool of light granted her by her lantern. Leaning over, she huffed a breath to snuff it out, waving her hand to dissipate the coil of smoke left behind. Pressing herself against the shelf, she cradled her staff against her chest and listened, all her senses on alert. Who was there? Her daughter? Or the Shadow Mage?

"Mother?" Her daughter's voice came again, accompanied by an unladylike oath, as she tripped over a chair in the darkness. Theda fumbled for her flint again, her lips quirking in the midnight gloom. That couldn't be the Dark Mage.

"Briana? I'm here." The light flared, and Briana stumbled into the space between the stacks, white-faced, tear-stained, and terrified.

Theda took a small step back as the girl flung her arms around her neck.

"Thank all the Gods, I was so hoping you would still be here. Mother, I'm sorry, so sorry."

Theda patted her heaving shoulder. "What has happened? How did you fight him off?" They both knew she wasn't referring to Darius.

"I've only got moments before he comes back. I snuck to your room. Took some of your potion, but there was not much there. Not enough to keep him off. I still don't know how I did it. I had to fight him all the way."

"I have more," Theda reached into the satchel for her supply. She showed it to Briana, who snatched it from her.

"I can't fight him. I'm so afraid Darius knows I am Blessed. We retired to our room for the night..." Briana blushed. "I ... was not myself. I think he knew."

"Where is he now?"

"Sleeping, I hope. Unless he was pretending."

She raised the flask, mouth open to drink, and winced as Theda batted her hand away.

"No. Not yet."

Briana's face whitened to the colour of snow. In the dim glow shed by the lantern, her eyes looked black. A skull. Theda shuddered.

"Please, I must..." She reached for the drug again, her hand trembling.

"First, we need to conceal the book of shadows. I've been trying to do it myself, but my magic does not work as yours does." Theda waved a tired hand at the book where it stood.

"My magic won't work on it either, not for long," Briana said. Her betrothal ring glinted in the light. "Please, mother. I'm so afraid of the Shadow Mage. I will give myself away to Darius. I know I will, and then Gods help us all. He already suspects you."

Theda stared at her. "Is that why you married him?"

Briana's eyes clouded with tears. "He said if I didn't marry him, he would see you to the gallows after Robert," she said.

Theda threw her hands in the air, flooded with remorse. "Oh, my dear. No. Why did you not tell me?"

Briana shrugged and swallowed. She stared at the floor. "I couldn't," she mumbled.

Theda surveyed her, sensing something untold. Her tidy, logical brain demanded explanations, but time was running out. Answers would have to wait.

"We must conceal the book, Briana. Help me. Quickly."

"What do you want me to do?"

"Give me your hand."

Eyes wide, Briana placed her small palm into Theda's rougher one. Swallowing heavily, Theda nodded at the heartsease tea. "Be ready with that, my dear. We are about to use a great deal of magic, and we may as well be shining like a lighthouse. The Shadow Mage will not be able to resist it."

Briana jerked her chin. "We'd better hurry. I can feel him stirring already."

"Alright. Breathe with me. We need to align our intent and purpose. We are sealing it with ancient magic, Briana. Blood magic. That's what will fix it permanently, so only our descendants will see it."

"Blood magic? Are you sure the Mage will allow it?"

"I sincerely hope so this time. It's the only option I have." Theda said, her voice grim. She slid her eating knife from its habitual place on her right hip. "Ready?"

"Do it."

Theda scored a slash in her own palm, and Briana winced when the sharp blade tore her own flesh. Their combined blood flowed onto the ancient cover, quickly absorbed by the cracked, dry leather.

"Mage, take our blood and fix our purpose, conceal this magic for those of our blood to know and use when the time is right. In you, we place our trust. Guard and protect our powers, in your name," Theda's voice pulsed, quiet and assured.

They waited, heads bowed, as Mage power hummed between them. Theda grimaced. Her previous attempts had depleted her. It was impossible to tell if the magic was working. She turned her head, alerted to the sound of the library door opening in the distance.

"Someone's coming. Quickly Briana, yours is the power to disguise and conceal. Use it now."

Briana's magic required no verbal urging. She closed her eyes, and beneath Theda's gaze, a new title appeared. The ornate scrawl in ancient ink crept across the formerly blank cover. "Of ye House of ye Eagle in ye Kyngdom of Epera". The pages rustled under their joined fingers, subtly rearranging themselves. Theda blinked as her daughter opened her eyes, and the mischievous gaze of the Dark Mage surfaced in their depths.

"Quick, Briana, make the book disappear!"

Briana gasped, her hands slipping away from her mother's frantic grasp. "I can't. He's coming!"

"Look at me, my love." Theda grabbed her hands, forcing them back to the book. "You can do this. I've got you, I won't let you go."

Her daughter squirmed, collapsing into herself as she fought the Shadow Mage for control of her mind. Agonised, Theda pushed strength into her with all the power she had left, conscious that it may not be enough. Footsteps approached. Confident and assured. More than one person. Soldiers. Her shoulders hunched. Fear scratched fingernails over her skin under her gown. Still some distance away, the footsteps halted, and she scowled, focusing on her daughter. Blocking them with difficulty from her conscious mind, she renewed her grip on Briana's slender hands, rough with drying blood.

"I can't do it!"

"You can. You must."

Breathing laboured, perspiration dotting her pale forehead, Briana took a deep breath, her face screwed in a mask of concentration. The atmosphere vibrated, quivering under the force of Briana's command. Mage power crackled under her skin. Theda let out a long sigh as the book vanished under her eyes. At the end of the stack, a new light appeared to join their own. Briana snatched the flask.

"If I drink this every day, in quantity, my magic will disappear. That's correct, isn't it?" she gabbled.

Theda nodded, mute with anxiety.

"And it will hold away the Shadow Mage, so none can see, find or use him?"

"That's right."

Briana nodded, her face grim, raised the flask and drank full and deep, her throat working as she gulped it down.

"Good evening, wife."

Commanding as iron, stiff with distaste, Darius's voice bled into the space between them.

Bloody hands still joined, they turned as one to face him.

His piercing dark eyes darted from their clenched fists stained with blood to their sombre faces, and his expression relaxed into something quite like satisfaction. As if he'd debated an academic point of detail and won. Impeccably dressed as usual, despite the lateness of the hour, he smoothed his tunic and allowed a shadow of his famous smile to creep across his face.

"I see my suspicion was correct about you all along," he said. "Witchcraft and blood magic. What an ill-judged combination. You surprise me, Mistress. I always believed you cleverer than that."

Briana's hand trembled in Theda's grip. Theda risked a glance at her as the Shadow Mage receded, and Briana slumped against her, face pale as parchment. One arm wound around her daughter, holding her close to her heart, Theda's gaze hardened.

"You may take me if you wish, but leave Briana alone," she said.

The young man's face twisted. "It will be the gallows for you. I will see to it. I will have no more of your kind in the kingdom. As for her, she is my wife. I will do with her whatever I want. A lifetime of pain will be the cost of her deception." He wheeled back into the library.

"Guard, arrest these women in the name of the King!"

Silence. Darius's voice rose to a roar of exasperation.

"Guard, why do you delay?" His angry footsteps receded.

Theda blinked at Briana's voice in her head, faint but more commanding than she had ever heard it.

"Darius of Falconbridge, you will never know this woman as my mother or the Seer of Epera. She is safe under your gaze, now and forever. And I am your faithful wife. Nothing more."

Her heart jumped at the instruction. *"Briana! You cannot conceal a person like that! It should not even be possible!"*

Grey eyes misted with tears and fatigue bored into hers. *"That is the last of my magic, fixed with our combined blood. We will never speak like this again. Not while Darius and the Shadow Mage exist in the same space."*

Theda blinked moisture from her eyes as her daughter smiled at her. *"The Mage is blessed in you," she said.*

"No, mother. This is a debt I owe." Briana's eyes slid away, full of regret, and Theda winced at the severing of their mental connection. A hollow thud of sadness drummed a funereal note in her chest, but she had no time to process it as Darius led a group of soldiers to the shelves and waved them forward.

"There is nothing to fear! Take the witch!" His voice was shrill, taut with tension.

Theda smoothed her face to a blank mask and concealed her grim smile as his expression shifted from dark anger into confusion. He frowned, rubbing his forehead as if to scrub away a dawning headache.

"Briana?" he said. "Who is this?"

The nearest soldier, Jacklyn Sommerton, turned into the light and winked at Theda.

He replaced his sword in its scabbard and shrugged his broad shoulders. "She's nothing, my lord, just a servant."

Darius nodded, his dark gaze bent possessively on his young wife. He took her hand to lead her away.

"You should be asleep. We leave for Falconridge in the morning," he said.

Briana let him tug her towards him, her eyes awash. Theda swallowed her anguish, struggling to play the role of placid servant Briana had constructed for her as their hands slid away, rough with their dried blood.

"Goodbye, my daughter, my brightling, my heart," she said in the depths of her mind.

Her daughter smiled, eyes sparkling like dewdrops in the lamp glow, even as her lips trembled.

"What are you doing here, anyway?" Darius continued, "I woke to find you gone."

Theda leaned on the shelf for support as they turned away, followed by the guard. Jacklyn nodded to her, his face grave and kind before he joined them.

"Just saying goodbye," Briana said. Her voice floated back like a phantom. An echo in the darkness, recorded by the library as their footfall faded.

Theda turned her face to the shelves and wept.

Epilogue

Castle of Air, 1573

Huddled in a new midnight black cloak, hugged tight against the unseasonal chill wind blowing from the mountains, Theda squinted into the late afternoon light through the fragrant smoke from her pipe. The carriage containing Queen Ariana rumbled away from her across the straw-dusted drawbridge. A small party of mounted soldiers wearing the grey and silver livery of the House of Wessendean clattered alongside it, their horses' hooves echoing from the harsh stone curtain wall.

"No more Ariana." At her side, Jacklyn Sommerton rolled his shoulders and shielded his eyes against the sun. Three years had broadened him further, and his cheeks bristled with the newly fashionable short beards sported by other young men at court. Married life suited him. Dora now worked at the Sign of the Falcon down in Blade.

"A long overdue decision," Theda said. "She'll do better away from the castle."

"Gossip says Falconridge refused to let her take her son. Did you hear that?"

"I did. Not that I'm surprised. Arion is the heir to the throne. There's no way Darius will let him out of his sight. Control means everything to him."

The two friends exchanged glances.

"Have you heard from Briana?"

"Of course. Jana is doing well. Looks just like her mother, from all accounts. As mischievous as her at the same age."

A smile tugged Jacklyn's mouth.

"Will you travel to see her?"

Theda glanced down at the trunk she'd packed the previous evening and then back to the courtyard, where a cart pulled by a sturdy horse lumbered forward to take her to Blade. The thickset driver pulled the conveyance to a halt, and the air was suddenly full of the essence of yeast and manure as the horse huffed a snort down her neck.

"Ready, Mistress?" he asked. "If we set off now, we'll be in Blade before dark."

Theda lowered her voice and looked up at Jacklyn. "To your father's place first, then onwards with the books."

She turned away from the carter and tipped her staff against Jacklyn's broad chest. A gentle hum of power throbbed through it, and his face creased into a grin.

"The Mage's blessing upon you, Jacklyn Sommerton," Theda said. She tapped her pipe out against the rough wood of the cart and stowed it with care in the pouch at her waist.

"And you, Mistress. Travel safe."

He offered an arm, and Theda clambered to a seat by the driver. Jacklyn hoisted her trunk over his shoulder and deposited it with a thump in the cart.

"All set," Jacklyn called.

Her driver jerked his chin and flicked the reins. Theda steadied herself against the jolt of the cart with her staff and faced forward to Blade.

Behind her, the castle starlings painted their age-old patterns across a lowering sky. And in the library, surrounded by the chatter of a new breed of scholar, shielded by ancient blood magic, a heavy book waited for the world to turn.

The End

Did you enjoy Seer of Epera? If you did, please go to the platform of your choice and help other readers discover and enjoy the world of Tales from the Tarot!

For updates, recommendations and giveaways, join my newsletter and get Carlos and the Mermaid, a FREE short story, set in Oceanis, the Kingdom of Cups. It's inspired by the tarot card Five of Cups. You can join my newsletter at https:/christinecazaly.com

Want to know who finds Theda's precious Book of Shadows?

Read **Queen of Swords**!

A kingdom lost to darkness

A failed queen tasked with bringing it to the light.

All Petronella had to do was give the dying kingdom of Epera an heir.

She failed.

Running for her life, Petronella is forced to confront the dark secrets of her past before a deadly and patient enemy gathers his forces to take her kingdom for himself.

But can she face her demons? Does she have the strength to claim her throne?

What will it take to become the true Queen of Swords?

If you adore tales of lost magic, high stakes and bittersweet endings, you'll love Queen of Swords.

Get it now!

Ebook version: from multiple platforms via this link or direct from my website at https://christinecazaly.com

Paperback version: from Amazon (UK, US and AUS) or direct from my website at https://christinecazaly.com (US and UK)

Follow me on:

Facebookhttps://facebook.com/christinecazalyauthor

GoodreadsChristine Cazaly (Author of Queen of Swords) | Goodreads

BookbubQueen of Swords (Tales from the Tarot) by Christine Cazaly - BookBub

Instagram https://www.instagram.com/christine_cazaly/

AmazonAmazon.com: Christine Cazaly: books, biography, latest update

Works in Progress

Page of Swords

A coming of age action adventure set in Epera featuring intrepid former stableboy Dominic Skinner. Battling to find his feet in Petronella's fledgling court, Dominic somehow loses her precious falcon. His desperate search for the missing bird leads him to treachery and intrigue – and the ultimate test of his own loyalty.

Projected release date October 2023

Knight of Wands

A fantasy adventure romance set in the scorching desert land of Battonia, as Domita Lombard fights for her right to love as she wills – and challenges her family, her society and her gods.

Projected release date March 2024

Join my newsletter for progress updates and to be notified when my next books are due for release!

AFTERWORD

The cards themselves inspire my standalone series Tales from the Tarot.

For the Tarot lovers amongst you, here are some clues for the cards that played strong character roles in Seer of Epera

Theda is an archetype, one of the Majors. She's the epitome of wisdom, but is not what you'd call a team player. Any idea which card might best represent her?

Darius. Studious, ambitious, determined and a force to be reckoned with. A character you would have to read as a reverse card. Which court card do you think fits him best?

Briana. Firey, charismatic, vibrant, but with a lot to learn. She's one of the court cards. But which one?

Robert Skinner. Erudite, charming, warm and friendly. Any ideas for the court card that best suits him?

And finally, there's one major arcana card that provides the overall theme for Seer of Epera. Which one do you think it is?

And here's a fun thing for you. I know the answers to these questions – but I'll put you down on my list for a FREE copy of Page of Swords if you email me with the correct answers!

ACKNOWLEDGMENTS

Many thanks to my editor, Natasha Rajendram of Scott Editorial for her kind words of encouragement and her ability to cut my sentences down to size. Gods know I need that! Ditto to the wonderful Taire of Tairelei.com for her beautiful cover design. I love the way you are helping to bring Tales from the Tarot to life.

Big hugs and hand claps for my beta readers Joy and Aly. I couldn't do this without your cheerleading and overall awesomeness. Shout outs for the wonderful authors who share their knowledge with such enthusiasm on the various facebook groups upon which I lurk. One day I'll feel worthy to contribute, but in the meantime, thanks for being such a great resource for all things self publishing. You guys rock!

And of course to my husband, and our expanding menagerie of animals. I love you all so much!

CC xx

Printed in Great Britain
by Amazon